THE JUST AND UNJUST

Lobo Lincoln—A special government agent, he's as wild and as tough as they come. Only one woman can tame him . . . and she's a woman worth killing for.

Jenny Moore—Beautiful and strong-willed, she knows just how cruel the West can be. But can she stand up to the likes of Gavin Brubaugh and his gang?

Gavin Brubaugh—Three hundred pounds of perversity, he kills for the sheer pleasure of it. He's got plans for Miss Jenny Moore, but they don't include killing . . . not just yet.

Ma Brubaugh—Gavin's mother, she taught him everything he knows. She wants to teach him one more lesson, and she'll use Jenny to do it.

Chief Iron Jaw—Leader of a band of renegade Shoshones, he's out to avenge the murder of one of his braves. He wants Brubaugh's blood and nothing can stand in his way.

The Stagecoach Series
Ask your bookseller for the books you have missed

STAGECOACH STATION 38:
GRAND TETON

Hank Mitchum

TM

BCI

Created by the producers of
**Wagons West, White Indian,
Badge,** and **Winning the West.**

Book Creations Inc., Canaan, NY · Lyle Kenyon Engel, Founder

BANTAM BOOKS
TORONTO · NEW YORK · LONDON · SYDNEY · AUCKLAND

STAGECOACH STATION 38: GRAND TETON
A Bantam Book / published by arrangement with
Book Creations, Inc.
Bantam edition / November 1988

Produced by Book Creations, Inc.
Lyle Kenyon Engel: Founder

ISBN 0-553-27546-1

Published simultaneously in the United States and Canada

Bantam Books are published by Bantam Books, a division of
Bantam Doubleday Dell Publishing Group, Inc. Its trademark,
consisting of the words "Bantam Books" and the portrayal
of a rooster, is Registered in U.S. Patent and Trademark
Office and in other countries. Marca Registrada. Bantam Books,
666 Fifth Avenue, New York, New York 10103.

PRINTED IN THE UNITED STATES OF AMERICA

KR   0 9 8 7 6 5 4 3 2 1

STAGECOACH STATION 38:

GRAND TETON

Grand Teton, Wyoming 1892

YELLOWSTONE NATIONAL PARK

Mt. Hancock

BOZEMAN

MONTANA

AREA SHOWN
ON MAIN MAP

WYOMING

LARAMIE

UTAH

COLORADO

BOULDER

Mt. Moran

Jackson Lake

TETON RANGE

Grand Teton

WYOMING MTS.

Upper Gros Ventre Butte

Gros Ventre Creek

Teton Pass

JACKSON

GROS VENTRE MTS.

Lower Gros Ventre Butte

0   5   10   20
MILES

Snake River

© BOOK CREATIONS INC. 1988

RON TOELKE '88

Chapter One

Although the morning sun was bright in the northwestern Wyoming sky on that mid-May day in 1892, the air had a cold bite to it, a reminder that winter had not been gone long from the high Rockies.

Heading north, a big, dark-skinned man on a sorrel gelding veered away from the banks of the Snake River to head toward the town of Jackson. As he rode, his dark brown eyes gazed across the broad southern sweep of the high desert valley called Jackson Hole, named for David E. Jackson, a fur trapper who had explored the valley more than a half century before. Smiling to himself, the rider remembered the first time he had come to this ruggedly beautiful country. Like countless others, he had gone searching for the hole itself—until he found out that "hole" was what trappers called a boxed-in valley.

Loping along, he saw that the grass in the valley was losing its tawny look, and tiny yellow-headed dandelions were beginning to bloom. Thin stalks of fireweed stirred in the soft May breeze, showing off their tight red crowns, which soon would burst open in a flaming display of color. Then the broad-shouldered rider took in the beauty of the lodgepole pines and the Douglas firs that fringed the valley and dotted the rolling hills. Shading his eyes, he let his gaze follow the magnificent Teton Range, stretching northward toward Montana.

The first time he had come to this country, he had fallen under the spell of these steep, lofty mountains.

1

Rising up out of the earth and taking a jagged bite out of the clear blue sky, the snowcapped peaks were an imposing sight.

The big man halted his horse and took a deep breath. No words could describe the splendor of the scene. The Tetons were the creator's handiwork at its best.

Reluctantly pulling his gaze from the awesome vista, he nudged the sorrel onward, and soon he topped a gentle rise to find Jackson spread out before him. Other villages dotted the valley, but Jackson, situated at the eastern base of the Gros Ventre Butte, had thrived to become a full-fledged town. He could see that many more buildings had been erected since he had passed through the area seven months before. Jackson had seen much progress.

The big man pulled up in front of Holland's General Store, dismounted, and tied his horse to the hitch rail. Standing beside his horse, he looked even more imposing than he had while still astride. Nearing thirty, the man stood six feet six in his boots and weighed a solid two hundred and fifty pounds. He was dressed in faded denim pants, a red flannel shirt, and a fringed buckskin jacket. Like many other men milling about on Jackson's dusty main street, he wore a pair of bone-handled Colt .45s slung low on his hips and a large hunting knife in a leather sheath strapped to his belt. But unlike most of the other men, he was fast and deadly with both weapons.

Lifting his broad-brimmed black hat and running fingers through his jet-black hair, he looked around and assessed the new business establishments. With his hat removed, the brilliant sunlight picked up the distinctive white scars on his right temple and cheekbone that contrasted with his swarthy skin. Despite the scars, the man was ruggedly handsome, and some female admirers had been known to say that the faint scars made his appearance all the more dashing.

As the towering figure stepped onto the boardwalk, a small boy stared up at him and, pointing a finger, exclaimed, "Mama, look at the giant! He's an Indian giant, Mama!"

"Shh!" chastised the young mother, her face coloring.

In a half whisper, she said, "Indians don't have mustaches, Timmy."

"But he's got red skin," the boy protested.

Lowering her head in embarrassment, the woman shepherded her outspoken son through the open doorway of the nearest shop.

The man looked after the mother and child and smiled, tugging on the end of his thick, black mustache. Then he pushed open the door of the general store, ducked his head, and went inside.

John Holland, the sixty-year-old proprietor, looked up from where he stood behind the long counter and smiled. "Ah, Lobo Lincoln!" he exclaimed. "Welcome back. It's good to see you again."

Looking down on the smaller man, Lobo smiled and said, "Thanks, Mr. Holland. It's good to be back in God's country."

Holland chuckled. "A lot of us feel that way about this area."

Lobo gazed around at the rows of canned and bottled goods, all neatly arrayed on the shelves. He nodded approvingly. "You've expanded your store since I was here."

"Had to," said the gray-haired proprietor. "Business is on the increase. I guess you noticed our little village is not so little any more."

"I sure did. There are two or three houses under construction just on this end of town."

"Uh-huh. Folks just keep moving in. Jackson's going to grow up to be a regular city one of these days, Lobo." Squinting and cocking his head, Holland asked, "What brings you back this way?"

"I'm on my way to the Flying M Ranch. When I was here last fall, George Muller offered me the foreman job. I thought I'd see if it was still open."

"As far as I know it is—leastways, I haven't heard of any new fellow at the ranch. I think George's boy, Steve, has been ramrodding for his pa, but I know he's been wanting to go back east to college." Holland paused. Looking somewhat surprised, he then asked, "You're really serious about this foreman job?"

"I sure am," Lobo said, looking around the shelves. "Say, where's your beef jerky, Mr. Holland?"

"Right over there," the shopkeeper replied, pointing toward a big glass jar at the end of the counter.

Unscrewing the lid and pulling out a fistful of jerky, the dark-skinned man asked, "Why did you ask if I was serious about the job?"

"Well, it's just that—"

The shop door opened, its bells jangling. "Good morning, Mr. Holland," a man said as he and his wife entered. The newcomers looked briefly at Lobo Lincoln and smiled tentatively.

"Good morning, Mr. Avery, Mrs. Avery. Beautiful day, isn't it?" the proprietor responded. "I'll be with you in a few moments. This fellow's come a long way, and he needs some assistance," Holland said, gesturing at Lobo.

"No, no, that's all right, Mr. Holland. Please take care of these folks first. I'm in no hurry," Lobo assured him.

He stood by the counter, watching Holland bustle around the store collecting the Averys' order. "Here, let me get that for you," Lobo said when the shopkeeper hefted a sack of flour to take to his customers' wagon. The Averys looked at him in amazement: Lobo lifted the hundred-pound bag with such ease that it might as well have been a feather pillow.

When Lobo was back inside and the Averys had gone, the shopkeeper turned his attention back to the big man. "Now, Lobo, what else do you need besides that jerky?"

"A couple boxes of .45s. I had a little run-in with some testy Utes down in Colorado and used up some of my reserve cartridges."

Taking the boxes of cartridges from a nearby shelf, Holland stacked them beside the beef jerky on the counter. "That reminds me of why I was surprised that you asked about that foreman job, Lobo. With all you've been doing for the past dozen years, from army scout to buffalo hunter to pathfinder—not to mention tracking down criminals as a special government agent—well, I wonder if you could really settle down to ranching."

"Well, yeah," Lobo said and grinned broadly. "I guess I have had a pretty exciting and adventurous past, haven't I?"

"Seems to me you'd get downright bored punching cattle and building fences."

Lobo chuckled. "Well, Mr. Holland, I can tell you that with the proper motivation, a man can do anything he sets his mind to."

Raising his bushy eyebrows, Holland said, "And you have that motivation?"

Pushing his hat to the back of his head, the big man grinned and said, "Sir, I have the best motivation a man can have for settling down in one place."

Holland looked slyly at Lobo and gave him a crooked smile. "You don't mean it."

"Yes, I do."

"Some little filly has thrown her lasso on big ol' Lobo Lincoln?"

"Frankly, I'm not sure who lassoed whom," Lobo said with a laugh, "but I'm definitely going to marry her and settle down."

"Well, tell me about her. Where's she from? What's she look like?"

Getting a dreamy look in his dark brown eyes, he replied, "Her name's Jenny Moore, and to say she's cute would be missing it by half. She's so beautiful, I sometimes think that maybe she's a goddess who fell to earth from another world. She's got honey-blond hair, and when the sun hits it, it looks like spun gold. She comes up to about here on me," Lobo said, gesturing to the top of his chest, "so I'd guess she's about five five—and she's as shapely a creature as you've ever seen."

"Sounds like Cupid has done a good job on you," Holland said with a laugh.

"No man ever got shot any harder," agreed Lobo.

"Well, I can't wait to meet her. Now, why don't you give me your list of supplies so I can fill it for you while you finish telling me about your Jenny."

"Okay. There're just a few more items," Lobo said as he handed Holland a slip of paper. He followed the shop-keeper around the store while the older man took things from his shelves. "Let's see," the big man said. "You wanted to know where Jenny's from, as I recall. She's from Indiana, and she was on a wagon train heading west through Colorado. I met her after her parents were killed when some Cheyennes attacked the train. She's living in Denver right now."

"Can she cook?" Holland said over his shoulder, grin-ning.

"Like a French chef," Lobo answered quickly. "This girl is everything a man could ever dream of, Mr. Hol-land. When God created the Tetons, He did a magnificent work—but when He created Jenny Moore, He did His masterpiece!"

"And you're going to settle down in Jackson Hole, you said?"

"That's my hope. The minute I find work that will keep me in one place, I'm going to send for her, and we'll be married."

"Congratulations, son," the shopkeeper said earnestly. "I sure hope it all works out for you."

John Holland was totaling the bill when the door opened and a tall, thin man in his early fifties came in. "Morning, Reverend," the shopkeeper said. "I'll be with you in a moment."

"Good morning, John," the preacher replied, his eyes taking in the massive form of Lobo Lincoln.

Noting the clergyman's response, the shopkeeper smiled and said, "This here grizzly bear is Mr. Lobo Lincoln, Reverend. Lobo, shake hands with the Reverend Thomas Carr."

"Glad to meet you, Reverend."

"Say, Reverend, I think I just drummed up some business for you."

"Oh?" said Carr, raising his thin eyebrows.

"Yep. Lobo is planning on getting married soon, and he and his bride are going to settle here in the valley."

"Well, congratulations, son," Carr said. "I would be

delighted to perform the marriage ceremony for you and your intended. You just let me know as soon as you've set a date."

"I sure will, sir. Thank you."

When the preacher had made his purchase and left, Lobo said to the shopkeeper, "I should be heading off, myself. It's good to see you again, Mr. Holland—and thanks for all your help."

"My pleasure, son," Holland replied. "Here, I'll take this package for you."

The two men stepped out into the bright sunlight, and Lobo stuffed the two packages of supplies into his saddlebags and then mounted his horse. Lobo's eyes were drawn to a store a few doors up the street, and he said to the shopkeeper, "I see you now have a telegraph office."

"Of course, son," Holland said, standing on the boardwalk. "We're seeing real progress here."

"Good," Lobo declared. "I hope I'll be needing to use that telegraph line real soon—to send that wire to Jenny." Smiling at the shopkeeper, he settled in his saddle for the two-hour ride to the Flying M Ranch, which was located to the east in the Teton Forest.

John Holland watched Lobo until he was out of town. As he turned to go back inside, he noticed four hard-looking men standing in front of the Elkhorn Saloon just up the boardwalk. They were staring at him cold-eyed with a look of annoyance. Giving them a casual glance, he went back into the store.

He was behind the counter adjusting some items on the shelves when the bell on the front door jangled. Holland looked over to see the four hardcases enter, their boots making shuffling noises on the wooden floor. Tiny needles pricked the shopkeeper's spine. He had a feeling these men were up to no good.

Three of the men were of medium height and stocky, with untrimmed beards and shabby attire. The fourth, a small, clean-shaven man, was wire-thin, and the sneer on his haggard face seemed to be etched there. At the end of his left wrist was a stump where a hand had once been. It

was the crazed look in his narrow, colorless eyes that put a
cold ball of fear in John Holland's stomach.

Stepping up to the counter with his cohorts flanking
him, the little man said in a high-pitched voice, "Did we
see what we think we saw, mister?"

"What do you mean?" asked Holland, trying to keep
his voice steady.

"Nobody plays dumb with Manfred Smith, mister!
Was that an Indian comin' out of this store carryin' goods
you sold him?"

Sweat beaded on John Holland's brow. The West was
full of white men who hated Indians, and some of them
considered it nothing short of treason for a white man to
befriend an Indian or act kindly toward one. Clearing his
throat slightly, Holland said, "If the man you're referring
to is Mr. Lobo Lincoln, yes, I . . . I believe he has some
Indian blood."

Manfred Smith leaned across the counter and snapped,
"So you *did* sell some goods to a stinkin' redskin."

"As I told you," said the gray-haired storekeeper,
"Mr. Lincoln is part Indian, but—"

Smith pulled his revolver from its holster. Thumbing
back the hammer, he said raggedly, "We don't cotton to
white yellow-bellied traitors who do business with Indians."

Holland held his breath, expecting a bullet to tear
into his body. When it did not come, he said nervously, "I
. . . I believe we have to take each man on his own merit,
Mr. Smith. Lobo Lincoln is a fine man. He—"

"Indians ain't got no merit!" Smith screamed. "They
ain't even human. They're *beasts* . . . beasts that oughtta
be exterminated like other filthy, scavenging animals."

While Holland stood frozen to the spot, Smith held
the gun on him and said to his cohorts, "Show Mr. Holland what we think of businessmen who deal with Indians,
boys."

John Holland felt sick as he was forced to stand and
watch as the three other men pulled all the neatly stacked
items off the shelves and threw them to the floor. Glass
articles shattered, and packaged goods were broken and
ripped open, their contents spilling out.

When the four men were satisfied that they had done enough damage, they trudged slowly toward the door, led by Smith. Pulling it open roughly, the little man snarled, "One word to anybody about who did this, Mr. Holland, and you're a dead man. But let it be a lesson to you: Don't do business with slimy redskins."

When the door was slammed shut, John Holland stared after the retreating men, the jarring sound of the bells reverberating in his ears. Silently wishing Jackson had a lawman, the shopkeeper sighed and set about cleaning up the mess.

It was just after four o'clock when Lobo Lincoln rode back into Jackson and hauled up in front of the Western Union office, which was merely a lean-to attached to the Wells Fargo Overland Stage Company building. Veering around the end of the hitch rail, he stepped up first to the Wells Fargo office. A note on the door indicated that the agent was not in, but next to it was posted a route schedule, which Lobo read carefully. Leaving the Wells Fargo door, Lobo ducked his head and entered the Western Union lean-to.

"Hello," he said to the telegraph operator. "I'd like to send two wires to Denver."

"Okay, young fella," the elderly man said, looking up at Lobo. "Fill out these forms with your message. Here's a pencil."

"Thanks."

The first telegram went to Jenny Moore, telling her that he was now foreman at the Flying M Ranch and that a beautiful log cabin went with the job. Jenny should give her notice at her job and take the Wells Fargo stage that would arrive in Jackson on June third. They would be married the day after she arrived, and he added that he already had a preacher lined up to perform the ceremony.

The second wire was to Mr. William Kettering at the Office of Territorial Affairs, announcing that he was resigning as a special agent of the U.S. government.

"Do you want to wait while I send these, young fella?" the operator asked.

"No, there's no need. Thanks."

Emerging from the lean-to, Lobo stepped back to the Wells Fargo office. The agent still had not returned, and this time Lobo read the note more closely. It said that agent Bob McGee was at the Elkhorn Saloon, and if his assistance was needed, come and fetch him.

Lobo was eager to book Jenny's seat on the stage, so he headed down the street toward the saloon. He was about to walk through the open door when he noticed John Holland sweeping up debris at the front of the general store. Waving a hand, he called out, "Hey, Mr. Holland! I got the job!"

Holland smiled and waved back. "Good, Lobo! I'm happy for you."

Going from the sharp glare of the sun into the relative gloom of the saloon, Lobo Lincoln was momentarily unable to see clearly, but his nostrils were immediately assaulted by the sharp odor of tobacco smoke, cheap whiskey, sour rum, and sweaty bodies. As his eyes finally adjusted to the small amount of light admitted by the open door behind him and two small windows at the back end of the room, he could see that the floor was covered with sawdust and the bar was just a couple of twelve-foot planks supported at either end by empty beer barrels on wooden blocks, making it barely more than waist high. There were a dozen crude tables, and instead of chairs the patrons sat on nail kegs.

As he looked around the dimly lit room, Lobo saw that about half the tables were occupied. Stepping over to the bar, he resisted the urge to duck as he walked under the beams that were just a foot from his head. He looked down at the fat, bald-headed bartender and smiled. "Howdy. I'm looking for Bob McGee, the Fargo agent. The note on his door said he'd be in here."

"Yessir," the man said and nodded, craning his neck to look Lobo in the eye. "He's over there playing poker at the table in the far corner. The guy in the white shirt with the string tie. Can I get you a drink?"

"No, thanks," Lobo replied. "I just need to do business with Mr. McGee."

As the towering, dark-skinned man threaded his way toward the far corner, he brushed past a table where four men sat drinking whiskey. One of them, the smallest, looked up at Lobo and said loudly to his friends, "I don't know about this town, boys. Not only do they sell their wares to dirty Indians, but they also let 'em into the drinkin' establishments."

Lobo heard the remark but ignored it. He was not looking for trouble, and he did not want to give the men the satisfaction of acknowledging their presence.

Approaching the corner table, he looked down at the agent, whom Lobo guessed to be in his early thirties. "Mr. McGee, I just stopped by your office and read the note on the door. I'd like to book passage for my future wife on the stage from Denver that will arrive in Jackson on June third."

Bob McGee was in the middle of dealing out cards, but after he had looked Lobo up and down, he put the deck down and said amiably, "Sure, mister. I wouldn't want to rile the likes of you by tellin' you to show up at the office later."

Lobo grinned. "I assure you that wouldn't rile me, Mr. McGee, and if you're too involved in the game, I can wait. I just would like to do my business before you close the office for the day."

Pushing back his chair, McGee said, "That won't be necessary, Mr.—"

"Lincoln. Lobo Lincoln."

"That won't be necessary, Mr. Lincoln. Business has to come before pleasure," he said, rising to his feet. "You boys chew the fat for awhile. I'll be back in a few minutes."

Lobo turned and headed for the door. As he reached the table where the four hardcases sat, the small, thin man rose and stood in Lobo's path, eyeing the big man defiantly. "You shouldn't be in here, Indian," he snarled. "You're stinkin' up the place."

Everyone in the saloon stopped and watched to see what Lobo was going to do. He felt his scalp go tight, and a slight flush showed at the base of his thick neck.

Seeing Lobo tense, Manfred Smith's three cohorts stood up and flanked their leader. Lobo looked each of them in the eye, then said quietly as he peered down at the waspish little man, "Sir, if you've had a bad experience with Indians, I'm sorry. But I bear you no ill will and I'm half Indian, so I don't see any cause for you to be alarmed."

Smith held up his purple stump and shook it in Lobo's face. "Your kind did this to me, redskin!" he choked angrily in his high-pitched voice. "You may be only half Indian, but as far as I'm concerned, you're a savage! Your bloody Shoshone did this to me!"

Lobo was aware that the man's three friends were slowly working their way around him. Keeping a tight rein on his emotions, he said in a steady voice, "I am not Shoshone, sir. I am Arapaho. I'm sorry for the loss of your hand, but I must ask you to step out of the way. This gentleman and I have business to take care of."

Smith abruptly shouted, "Get him, boys," and he whipped out a hunting knife.

Reacting with the ferocity and speed of a cornered cougar, Lobo kicked Smith violently in the stomach. The man crumpled to the floor in agony, lying screaming on the sawdust-covered floor with his knees pulled up to his face.

A second man swore at Lobo and charged at him with his knife bared, but Lobo grabbed the man's wrist and twisted it loose. As the knife hit the floor, Lobo leapt at the man, looping his fingers into his shirt and belt and throwing him over the table into the third man. The two of them slammed into an empty table, smashing it to pieces, and ended up on the floor, a mass of tangled arms and legs.

The man who'd had the knife grabbed it up from the floor and came at the big man again. But Lobo, who had been forced to fight like this before, was already bringing up a heavy-booted foot, and it caught the man's knife hand, sending the long-bladed weapon sailing harmlessly across the room. Seizing the man's shirtfront, Lobo drove a rock-hard fist into his jaw, knocking him out cold.

"Look out, Mr. Lincoln!" Bob McGee yelled.

Lobo whirled around to find himself facing a drawn revolver held by the other thug. Moving like lightning, Lobo whipped his own gun out and fired, drilling the man through the heart.

The bartender and his patrons all watched Lobo in slack-jawed amazement. Ignoring their awed expressions, he casually stooped over and picked up his hat, popping it back into shape and dusting it off against his thigh. As he placed it on his head, he walked over to Manfred Smith, who still lay doubled up on the floor, gagging from the pain.

Looming over Smith, Lobo spoke to him in a low, even voice. "I try to be a peaceful man, but when somebody pulls a knife or a gun on me, I get mean. Don't ever get in my way again."

Lobo turned on his heel and, with McGee, exited the saloon, leaving the bartender and his patrons whispering about the size, strength, and speed of the man with the curious name.

Chapter Two

Some two hundred miles away, in the far northwest corner of Colorado, a special stagecoach bearing Colorado's governor, Roger Whitson, was making its way toward Steamboat Springs. Once it had reached its destination, a violent incident would occur.

The state was suffering from political unrest. Many citizens were blaming Whitson for Colorado's problems, and the governor felt that a whistle-stop tour via stagecoach might help reassure his constituents that not only were those problems going to be solved, but that he was the one to solve them—thereby assuring himself another term, come election day in November. Steamboat Springs was his final stop on a trip that had crisscrossed Colorado for the past ten days.

Barely aware of the beautiful landscape moving slowly past the windows of the coach, Whitson sat in a plush, overstuffed seat of the specially outfitted stagecoach, puffing on a big black cigar and gazing at the gaunt face of his aide, Hector Wesley, who sat in the seat opposite. Two bodyguards also occupied the coach. Speaking past the cigar between his teeth, Whitson said, "I'm glad this tour is just about over with, and I'm pleased with our results. I believe that the reaction from the people is far more supportive after my speeches than the attitude they show before I get started."

Hector Wesley looked over his glasses and said levelly, "I think the reaction of the people has gotten the

14

message across to your competitor. He can't be too pleased with the success of this tour."

A look of outrage leapt into Whitson's eyes. "Hah!" he crowed. "Albert Overby couldn't whip me in the last election. What makes him think he can do it in the next one?"

"I certainly agree, Governor," Wesley said, adding cautiously, "but he *has* swayed a good many people to his position in the last few months, and I think he'll be harder to beat next time."

Whitson swore and flicked the ashes of his cigar angrily. Glaring at his aide, he growled, "The only way Albert Overby can become the next governor of Colorado is over my dead body." The governor glanced at his two bodyguards sitting opposite each other next to Wesley and himself. "And I'm counting on you two to ensure that that remains just a figure of speech!"

The two men smiled at Whitson and patted their rifles reassuringly.

Hector Wesley cut in, throwing his palms up. "Gentlemen! You act as if we lived fifty years ago. The West is quite civilized now. Albert Overby is a politician, not an assassin. He'll do his attacking from his political platform, using his best weapon . . . his mouth. He is not going to resort to violence."

Shuffling through some papers, the governor said, "How much longer until we reach Steamboat Springs?"

"About forty minutes, sir."

"That's all? Good heavens! Quickly, Wesley, let's add something a bit more dramatic to my speech this time. I want this tour to end with a real bang!"

By nine-thirty that morning a sizable crowd had gathered at the depot in Steamboat Springs, where Governor Roger Whitson's private stagecoach would soon arrive. The depot had been selected as the best site for the rally because its yard was large enough to accommodate such a crowd. The wooden platform from which the governor would speak was draped with red, white, and blue bunting. Political arguments were going on among a dozen or more spectators, and a few tempers were flaring when Bart Kemp, alone and on horseback, drifted into town. As he headed down the main street, his eyes roved back and forth, looking for a particular face.

He pulled up at the side of the depot and dismounted, circling around the building and searching the crowd intently. When he did not see the person he was looking for, he returned to the spot where he had left his horse.

Kemp paced nervously beside his mount as Steamboat Springs's citizens continued to arrive from every direction. Entire families strolled toward the station, which had been made festive with tricolored streamers. Dozens of flags were being waved by the crowd, who seemed to be treating this political rally with the same holiday spirit as a trip to the county fair.

Kemp watched the youngsters gamboling about. Although the thought of children and babies being vulnerable to stray bullets was distasteful to him, he told himself that he had no choice; he had agreed to arrange this mission. With Roger Whitson dead, Kemp's friend Albert Overby would have a clear path to the governor's mansion—and he, Bart Kemp, would be a high-paid, high-ranking adviser to the new governor.

Kemp pulled a gold watch from his vest pocket. "Fifteen more minutes," he mumbled. "Where's Brubaugh? We've got to have some time to go over the plan. If he doesn't—"

He cut his mumbling short when he saw six riders round the corner a block away and head for the depot. He could tell by the size of the lead rider that it was Gavin Brubaugh. A minute later, Brubaugh and his five tough-looking men drew up alongside Kemp and dismounted.

Bart Kemp stared at Brubaugh, thinking as he always did that this giant was probably the homeliest man he had ever seen in his life. His appearance alone would frighten most people into giving the man what he wanted. Standing six feet six inches and weighing a meaty three hundred pounds, Brubaugh had on scruffy bib overalls and a dirty plaid flannel shirt, and belted to his ample waist was a holster that bore a big .45-caliber Dragoon revolver. His pale blue eyes were set far apart, and he had a broad, flat nose and huge purple lips, which peeked out of his long, unkempt beard.

Brubaugh briefly lifted his wide-brimmed hat in greeting as he stepped close to Kemp. "Howdy. Looks like we're right on time."

"I was getting worried," Kemp said a bit tartly. "I thought you'd already be here when I rode in."

"No sense in worryin'," Brubaugh replied, his voice deep and gravelly. "With all that money in the offin', ol' Gavin ain't gonna fail to show up."

"Okay." Kemp nodded. "Gather your boys around. Let's make sure you know exactly what you're to do."

"You don't have to worry about that, either," said Brubaugh. "My ma masterminded the whole thing, and when Ma Brubaugh works it out, it ain't gonna flop."

Bart Kemp nodded silently, maneuvering himself so that he was obscured from any onlookers. He did not want anyone to connect him with the gang.

Brubaugh, looking down on the smaller man, asked, "Did you find out anything about Whitson's bodyguards?"

"Yes, he has two of them. And, incidentally, while I was waiting, I noticed the county sheriff and his deputy standing near the platform, keeping their eyes on the crowd." He gave Brubaugh a sidelong glance and cleared his throat. "I'm sure you know what you're doing, but I'd like to hear your plan, just to be reassured—that is, if you don't mind," he added quickly.

"Nah, I don't mind. We've got some time to kill— before we do some *real* killin'," Brubaugh said, and then he guffawed. Gathering his five men close in, he said, "Boys, let's go over this stuff for the last time."

Bart Kemp tried to ignore the pungent smell of the six unwashed bodies as he listened intently.

"Okay," Brubaugh grunted to his men, "now Ma's been to this kind of gatherin' before, and she says the lawmen usually stand at the back of the platform, facin' the crowd. But even if they're somewheres else, they gotta be killed instantly."

Kemp noted that Brubaugh's motley bunch seemed to light up at the thought of killing.

Starting at his left, the gang leader said, "Neal, what's your job?"

Neal Shaffer replied quickly, "I'll stand right next to you, Gavin. You'll call the governor a liar, and that's my signal to go for my guns. Then you and me are gonna shoot the governor."

"Right," grunted the huge man. Looking at the next outlaw, he said, "Okay, Herman, what's your part in this?"

Herman Tarver snapped in response, "I'm to be standin' a bit to your left, Gavin, and my job is to shoot the bodyguard who's standin' to the governor's right."

"How many times are you supposed to shoot him?"

"Till he's dead."

"You got it." To the next man in the circle, Brubaugh said, "Bill, where are you gonna be, and what're you gonna do?"

"I'm gonna stand off to your right," came Bill Kopack's reply, "and I'm gonna drill the bodyguard what's standin' to the governor's left. And I'm gonna *keep* drillin' till he don't move no more."

"And when are you two gonna shoot these bodyguards?" asked Brubaugh.

"The same time you and Neal shoot the governor," replied Kopack.

Looking to the next man, Brubaugh said, "Carl, how about you?"

Carl Blade spit a brown stream of tobacco juice and answered, "I'm gonna be standin' so that no matter where the sheriff is, I can kill him dead at the same time you and Neal let the governor have it."

Satisfied with Blade's reply, Brubaugh looked at the last man. Fred Foss grinned and said, "I'm to be standin' where I can drop the deputy when you other guys are doin' your killin'."

"Okay," said Brubaugh, satisfied. He looked at Bart Kemp to make sure he was suitably impressed. Then he said to his gang members, "Ma said some of the men in the crowd will probably pull guns. What'll we do about that?"

Fred Foss spoke up. "As soon as me and Carl have cut down the two lawmen, we're supposed to grab the two closest younger-type women and put our guns to their heads. At the same time, we're to shout at the crowd that if anybody tries to shoot us, we'll kill the women."

"Good," declared Brubaugh. Looking at the others, the huge man said, "Now, if somehow Carl or Fred takes a bullet, we still got to grab two women, like Ma said. So be watchin' close, understand?"

The others nodded.

"Why do you have to take two innocent bystanders?" Kemp asked, clearly uncomfortable with the notion.

"The women will be hostages. We've got two extra horses with us just for them."

"But you'll turn them loose once you're safely out of the area, of course?"

"Naw," said the huge, ugly man, shaking his head and grinning. "Ma wants us to bring one of 'em to the hideout. She always likes to have a young woman around to do the housework and the cookin'. A slave, Ma calls her."

"You don't have a, uh, slave at the hideout now?"

"Nope. Betty Mae hanged herself. So we gotta bring Ma another one."

Kemp swallowed hard. "What about the other woman? You said you're only taking one to the hideout."

"We'll kill her," Brubaugh replied callously.

Bart Kemp went cold all over. He really did not like being involved in such things. The slave idea was horrible, but the killing of the second woman was worse. He wished Gavin Brubaugh had not told him about it.

"Anyway," Brubaugh spoke up, "we'll meet you at the same place we met when you hired us—at that old shack just across the Wyoming border."

"Right," said Kemp. "I'll stay here in town for a short while after you've gone. We shouldn't do anything that could cause somebody to connect us." He did not tell

Brubaugh that he wanted to make sure Whitson was actually dead before he paid the gang leader.

A chuckle came from deep in Gavin Brubaugh's throat. "Yeah, I understand. That bein' the case, I'd suggest you saunter as far away from the action as possible. 'Cause before you know it, ol' Whitson'll be deader'n a rusty old doornail, and I sure wouldn't want you accidentally gettin' hurt in the fracas that's gonna follow."

Kemp nodded in agreement, and looking carefully around to make sure no one was watching him, he slipped away to the back of the crowd.

Gavin Brubaugh turned to his men and said, "Okay, boys, let's get ready." Moments later, Brubaugh and his gang were mingling in the crowd in front of the depot.

Soon someone shouted, "Here she comes!"

All discussions stopped, those that were heated as well as those that were friendly, as everyone watched the stagecoach roll toward them. Sheriff Ed Anderson and his deputy stepped toward the platform, where the coach would pull to a halt. Under the watchful eyes of Carl Blade and Fred Foss, the two lawmen instructed the crowd to step back from the area surrounding the platform to give the coach plenty of room.

Gavin Brubaugh noted the position of the sheriff and deputy. Then, irritating many in the crowd, he pushed his bulk through to a place that would allow him to get a good shot at the governor. Brubaugh made sure that a row of observers was standing in front of him; they would shield him sufficiently to keep the governor, his bodyguards, and the lawmen from seeing him draw his gun. Neal Shaffer followed closely in his boss's wake and stood next to him. Meanwhile, Bill Kopack and Herman Tarver also shouldered their way through the crowd to take their assigned places.

The hubbub increased as the stagecoach drew nearer, and soon the noise was almost deafening. When the coach had come to a halt, the sheriff and his deputy stepped close to the door as the two bodyguards emerged through it. The crowd pushed closer behind the lawmen in order to get a good look at the governor and hear what he had to say. Brubaugh and his men moved with the flow of the crowd, maintaining their positions.

The governor's bodyguards scanned the crowd and then stepped over to speak to the two lawmen. Gavin Brubaugh could not hear what they were saying, but while they talked, he looked around to make sure each of his men was in his place. They were ready.

Then one of the bodyguards went back to the open door of the coach and spoke to someone inside, and moments later Hector Wesley appeared, and the rumbling voices of the crowd quickly died out. The aide followed the sheriff and deputy the few yards to the platform stairs, which they all quickly mounted. Turning to the crowd, Wesley said, "Ladies and gentlemen, we are delighted to see how many of you have gathered here today to see and hear your governor."

There were many cheers and some boos.

Wesley raised his hands, calling for quiet, and continued. "Governor Whitson is taking his valuable time to make these whistle-stop appearances all over our state because he loves the people of Colorado and he feels he owes it to you as your leader to clarify personally some of the issues that have you all concerned." Pausing for effect, Wesley pasted on a wide smile, then said, "And now, ladies and gentlemen, the man you are all waiting to hear. I give to you your governor, the Honorable Roger Whitson!"

Gavin Brubaugh and his men tensed as Whitson came through the stagecoach door and climbed down. Followed by the two bodyguards, he stepped briskly to the platform, climbed the stairs, and joined his aide and the lawmen. At the rear of the crowd, Bart Kemp's heart quickened pace. Sheriff Anderson and his deputy stood alert at the rear of the platform, their hands on the butts of their holstered guns, while the bodyguards, who flanked Whitson, watched the crowd with piercing eyes, holding their carbines ready.

At the governor's appearance there had been a loud roar from the crowd, a commingling of cheers and a few catcalls. Whitson raised his hands to quiet the crowd, but it took the better part of a minute before he could finally begin his speech.

Slowly Gavin Brubaugh's men placed their hands on their guns. Brubaugh watched and listened carefully, waiting for just the right moment to pull off the assassination. He had not known about the governor's aide, but the little man did not appear to be much of a threat.

Whitson had the attention of the entire throng as he settled into his speech. There were some low murmurings among the people, but for the most part, the audience stood rapt.

Suddenly drawing his gun and thumbing back the hammer, Gavin Brubaugh shouted, "Whitson, you're a dirty liar!"

Brubaugh's gun roared, and the slugs ripped through the governor, immediately followed by two shots from Neal Shaffer's revolver. The impact of the three bullets slammed Whitson back a few feet, and then he fell, slumping into a chair on the platform, his arms dangling.

There was instant bedlam in the crowd. Women began screaming, men were shouting, and children were crying. Some people dropped to the ground to keep from getting hit, and others began to flee the scene. Among them was Hector Wesley, who had jumped from the platform with the first crack of a bullet and was now running for his life.

Then Herman Tarver and Bill Kopack opened fire on the bodyguards, and the bystanders grew even more frantic.

Just before Herman Tarver's targeted bodyguard took two bullets, the man saw Neal Shaffer's gun come up to fire again. Reacting instinctively, he shot at Shaffer, hitting him in the left side, and Shaffer went down with a howl. Tarver then fired two shots, which buckled the bodyguard but did not kill him. As the carbine slipped from the bodyguard's hands, he managed to reach inside his coat for one of his revolvers. But Tarver fired again, twice, and one slug tore into the bodyguard's temple, while the other hit him in the throat. The man stiffened, peeled forward onto the edge of the wooden platform, and landed on the ground below in a crumpled heap.

The other guard was even harder to kill than his partner. Bill Kopack fired two shots, one of which went in the man's chest, but the bodyguard did not fall. The impact of the hot lead drove him backward into a wooden post, but the wounded guard quickly regained his balance and brought his carbine to bear. But just as he was ready to fire, a terror-stricken woman stumbled in front of Kopack, and the guard hesitated.

Gavin Brubaugh, seeing what was happening, turned his smoking gun on the bodyguard and fired. Although the gallant bodyguard was hit again, he still refused to go down, raising the carbine to fire at Brubaugh. Then two more of Bill Kopack's bullets hit him, and he jerked from the impact, causing the shot from his carbine to go wild. The .44-caliber slug hit a woman thirty feet away who was attempting to escape the melee, and she staggered and then fell to the ground screaming. The bodyguard fell to the platform's floor, his body smeared with the blood his dying heart was pumping through the bullet holes.

While all this was going on, Carl Blade and Fred Foss had unleashed their guns on the sheriff and his deputy. Both lawmen were hit just as they were drawing their revolvers. The deputy fell from the platform with his gun blazing, but the shot went wild. Foss's bullet had hit him in his head, killing him instantly.

Sheriff Ed Anderson staggered when he was hit by two bullets, but he managed to get off a shot at Carl Blade. As the bullet whizzed by Blade's head, the outlaw ducked instinctively, throwing his aim off when he fired again at the sheriff. Both bullets missed Anderson, one tearing into the already dead body of the governor, dangling over the chair. Then Anderson collapsed from the effect of Blade's initial shots.

While most of the townspeople had fled or taken cover, some had pulled their guns to fire back at the assailants. Now two of them, standing some twenty-five feet apart, fired quickly at the biggest target they could see . . . Gavin Brubaugh.

Brubaugh felt the cross-whip of hot lead on both sides of his face as the bullets whizzed by him. Adept with a gun in either hand, the huge man whirled around and cut first one man down, then the other.

Herman Tarver saw a man inside the depot move to a window and raise a rifle. He put two shots through the window, and the man disappeared.

By this time, Carl Blade and Fred Foss were looking around at the women, both those fleeing and those prostrate on the ground, trying to find the right ones to take as hostages. Suddenly Blade saw a woman with fiery red hair crawling along the tracks. He ran over to her and gripped her arm, jerking it hard. She looked up at him with fear-filled eyes, and the outlaw guessed from her somewhat plain face that she was around thirty.

"You'll do," he grunted to the horrified woman, dragging her to her feet. Blade snapped back the hammer of the gun in his right hand as he locked her neck in the crook of his arm. Pressing the muzzle to her head, he shouted at the townsmen who were firing at the gang, "Every one of you, drop your gun!"

When the men of Steamboat Springs saw the danger that their neighbor Dora Phillips was in, they instantly obeyed.

Grabbing a pretty young brunette who was inching her way to the depot, Fred Foss held his gun to her head, threatening to shoot her if she did not stop screaming. Foss smiled wickedly as he appraised her, satisfied with his choice. Ma Brubaugh would be pleased.

Dragging the brunette over to where Gavin Brubaugh stood, Foss hollered at the townsmen, "No one makes a move toward us or these women will die! Do you all understand that?"

The townsmen wordlessly nodded their heads, feeling completely helpless.

"Good work, boys!" called out Brubaugh. "Let's go."

From where he knelt beside the wounded Neal Shaffer, Bill Kopack called, "Gavin, Neal's been hit!"

Brubaugh turned and looked at Shaffer. There was a pool of blood beside him. "Where're you hit?" Brubaugh asked him gruffly.

Through clenched teeth, Shaffer said tightly, "In the side."

"Can you ride?"

"Gavin, he's bleedin' pretty bad," Kopack argued.

"I asked him if he could ride," Brubaugh said curtly.

"Yeah," grunted Shaffer. "I think so. But it might be best if you just leave me here. I don't want to slow you down."

Bill Kopack's face stiffened. "We ain't leavin' you here, Neal. You can make it. We'll get you to the hideout and fix you up." Kopack instantly began to tear at Shaffer's shirt and stuff it against the wound. "Maybe that'll slow down the bleedin'," he declared.

Brubaugh looked around at the bodies of the governor, his bodyguards, and the two lawmen, pleased that everything had gone just as they had planned. Then he turned to the handful of terrified onlookers who remained. He barked, "I want all of you out of my sight! If you ever want to see either of these women alive again, I better not see anybody on the streets when we're ridin' out, 'cause if anybody follows us, these two are dead!" Waving his guns at the townspeople, he snarled, "Go on! Get out of here!"

The people quickly cleared the depot and the streets while the outlaws got their horses. Bill Kopack helped the wounded Neal Shaffer mount up, and then he brought the two horses around for the hostages to ride.

"Okay, boys," Brubaugh said. "Get those two females on their horses."

"Where are you taking us?" demanded the young brunette, tears streaming down her face.

"You'll find out," Brubaugh replied tartly. "You just do what you're told, and you won't make me put a bullet through your pretty head."

After forcing the women onto their designated horses, the gang mounted up. The women looked at each other with despair. Just then a middle-aged man came out of a shop across the street from them and called to Gavin Brubaugh, "Hey, mister!"

Fury turned Brubaugh's face as red as brick dust. "I said off the streets!" he bellowed.

"Please, mister," pleaded the man, walking closer. "If you need a hostage, why don't you let Dora and Lois go and take me?" Stepping even closer, the man continued, "Please, mister. A hostage is a hostage, so why not a man instead of two women?"

Gavin Brubaugh raised his gun to waist level and pointed it at the man's belly. "The only reason I don't shoot you on the spot is because I admire a man with guts. But if you don't disappear from my sight in the next five seconds, I'm gonna spill those guts of yours all over the street—and I'm warnin' you, I ain't kiddin'."

The look in Gavin Brubaugh's hard eyes showed the man that he meant it. As he turned and ran back toward the building, the brunette called after him, "Bless you, Charlie!"

"Let's ride!" Brubaugh shouted, and in a cloud of dust, the gang and their hostages rode hard out of Steamboat Springs, heading north for the Wyoming border.

The townspeople started pouring into the street, hurrying back to the station to take care of the wounded and the dead. "Look!" one of the men shouted. "Sheriff Anderson's still alive! Somebody go get Dr. Bailey!"

Ed Anderson lived long enough to tell the men who surrounded him that the big gang leader was Gavin Brubaugh. "Wire William Kettering at the U.S. Office of Territorial Affairs in . . . in Denver," he whispered. "He's . . . got to get a U.S. marshal on Brubaugh's trail. That . . . that assassin . . . has to be caught."

Anderson died within minutes.

After doing what their sheriff had ordered, the angry townsmen, ignoring the warning of the gang, formed a posse. In the light of the late afternoon sun, the corps of men thundered out to trail the bloody killers and rescue the two young women.

Chapter Three

Their horses were panting and flecked with foam as the Brubaugh gang finally crossed the Wyoming border north of Steamboat Springs, Colorado. Holding the exhausted animals at a hard gallop, the gang rode another two miles and then dropped over the top of a grassy hill, where Gavin Brubaugh abruptly reined in.

While the others jerked their mounts to a standstill, Gavin Brubaugh slid from his saddle and ran back to the top of the south-facing hill.

"What are you doin', Gavin?" Bill Kopack hollered after him.

The big man called back, "I want to see if there's a posse after us. And if there is, I want to see if they'll cross the border."

The rest of the gang dismounted, except for Neal Shaffer, who was bent over in his saddle, bleeding profusely. Kopack and Herman Tarver went over to check on him while Carl Blade and Fred Foss made sure the women's hands were still securely tied. The women looked sadly at each other, trying to give encouragement to one another with their eyes.

At the top of the hill, Gavin Brubaugh looked across the plains, watching for movement in the light of the waning sun. After nearly twenty minutes, he saw a dust cloud, and soon the posse came into focus. He could count sixteen horses as, suddenly, the riders stopped short. They had reached the border.

The sixteen men dismounted and paced back and forth for several minutes, apparently discussing whether or not to venture across the state line. Brubaugh knew that when it came to an arrest, the posse could not touch them in Wyoming; the question would be whether they would continue on anyway to try to rescue the women.

Brubaugh was relieved when he saw them turn and ride back toward Steamboat Springs. Wheeling around, he descended the hill, and when he reached the bottom, he told his men they were no longer being pursued. They, too, showed relief.

Kopack approached his leader and said, "Gavin, Neal's in pretty bad shape. So long as we ain't bein' followed, maybe we'd better rest here for a while before we go on to the shack."

Brubaugh stubbornly shook his ponderous head. "We're goin' to the shack right now," he grunted. "Kemp will probably take another route to meet us—after all, it'd look a mite suspicious to that posse if they was to meet up with him. He's circling around them, most likely, so he won't come by here. The shack's only another couple of miles. Mount up. Let's go."

Kopack's eyes sharpened as if he was going to say something, but he held his peace. Instead, he spoke a comforting word to his wounded cohort and then swung into his saddle.

A half hour later, the gang rode into a thicket-covered ravine and followed it about three hundred yards to an old shack nestled in a stand of pines. A small brook gurgled nearby, and when everyone had dismounted, Foss and Blade led the horses to it and let them drink. Kopack and Tarver carried Neal Shaffer into the shack and laid him on an old cot.

Brubaugh had untied the two women and pushed them into the ramshackle building, forcing them to sit on dusty wooden chairs. Looming over them, Brubaugh demanded, "What're your names? Either one of you married?"

The redhead's hazel eyes reflected the fear racing through her body. Hesitantly, she answered, "M-my name is Dora Phillips, and I . . . I am a widow. My husband was killed two years ago."

The gang leader eyed the woman and growled, "What's your age?"

"Th-thirty two."

"Kinda old," the ugly man grumbled. Looking down at the pretty brunette, he demanded, "What about you?"

Staring up at him, she said defiantly, "My name is Lois Crane, and I am not married."

"How old are you?"

"Twenty-two."

Exposing a mouthful of yellow teeth, Brubaugh grinned slyly and said, "You're real good lookin'. How come you're not married?"

Lois's dark brown eyes grew colder. "It's bad enough you've taken us against our will. I don't have to answer your impertinent questions!"

Still grinning, Brubaugh looked around at his men and declared, "Looks like we've got a female with a bit of sass in her system. Ma might have some fun knockin' it out of her."

The outlaws guffawed heartily, elbowing each other in the ribs.

Lois Crane stared unwaveringly at the huge man and asked, "Why are you asking us all these questions? What difference could it possibly make? Aren't you going to let us go now that the posse has turned back?"

"No, ma'am," Brubaugh replied bluntly. "We ain't lettin' you go."

Lois's brow furrowed, and a shiver went through her body. "What are you going to do with us?"

"You'll find out soon enough," Brubaugh grunted in his deep gravelly voice. Then he pivoted and walked away.

Dora sucked in a shaky breath and let out a whimper. Lois, looking at the older woman, gently patted her hand. "We'll be all right," she said softly, wanting to believe her own words. "We'll get out of this somehow."

Bill Kopack came into the shack and moved past Lois Crane, nearly brushing into her. Almost without thinking, Lois reached out and grabbed the gun from his holster.

But Kopack was too fast and too strong. He closed his

fingers around her wrist and bore down hard, and she let
go of the gun. Kopack eased up with the pressure as he
took the gun and dropped it back in the holster, but he
did not release Lois's wrist.

She looked up at him with scorn and demanded, "Let
go of me!"

Eyeing her with open appreciation for her beauty, he
said with a smirk, "I'll let go of you when I'm good and
ready. You shouldn't be tryin' to take a man's gun away
from him, sweet thing. You could get your arm broke that
way." He paused, still holding her wrist firmly, then chuckled. "Gavin's right. You do have some sass in you. Since
that sass comes from your pretty mouth, I think I oughtta
fix it so's you can't speak—like by kissin' you long and
hard."

"Let go of her, Bill!" Brubaugh snapped.

Kopack looked over at the huge man. "Aw, Gavin, I
was just—"

"Now!" Brubaugh shouted.

Kopack let go of Lois and walked to the other side of
the shack, while Brubaugh stomped over to the young
woman. "Don't try anything like that again, lady. Not if
you know what's good for you. I—"

At the sound of hoofbeats outside, all heads turned,
and the outlaws whipped out their guns, training them on
the doorway.

"It's probably Kemp," said Brubaugh. "But if it ain't,
whoever he is, he's a dead man."

A familiar voice called out, "Brubaugh! It's Bart Kemp!"

Brubaugh's massive frame crossed the floor. He pulled
open the door, gun in hand. Reassured that Kemp was
alone, he holstered his revolver and said, "Come on in."

"It took me longer than I'd planned," Bart Kemp said
as he entered the shack and closed the door behind him.
"I had to dodge the posse that was after you. I guess you
know they followed you to the border, then gave it up."

"Yeah," Brubaugh said and grinned. "I sure am glad
Wyomin' became a state a couple years ago and has its
own lawmen."

"So am I," responded Kemp, his eyes settling on the

women. Again, he wished that he did not know what was going to happen to them.

Brubaugh said, "Did you stick around long enough to find out if Whitson was dead before you lit out, Bart?"

Turning to face him, Kemp answered, "Yes, I did. I watched them take his body off the platform."

"Was he dead enough for you?"

"Quite."

"You got the money?"

Reaching into his coat, Kemp pulled out a brown envelope. As he handed it to Brubaugh, he said, "You tell your ma the whole thing was very well thought out. All you boys did a good job." Sending a glance Neal Shaffer's way, he added, "Sorry he was wounded. Is he going to be all right?"

Kopack stood at Shaffer's side and answered, "Sure, Mr. Kemp. Neal's gonna be okay."

Moving over to the table, Brubaugh sat down and began to count the money.

"What's the matter, Gavin?" asked Kemp, moving close. "Don't trust me?"

"It ain't that at all," grunted the big man. "But you're human, and you might not've counted right. If I show up at the hideout with less than I'm supposed to, Ma will skin me alive."

Bart Kemp waited until Brubaugh had finished the count, then said, "Well, I appreciate all you've done for us. Now Albert Overby is certain to become Colorado's next governor, and yours truly has been promised a high-paying position with him." Kemp suddenly realized that his name and the name of the mastermind of the assassination had now been revealed to the two women, and he stared at them, his face hardening. Then he relaxed, reminding himself that there would be no way they could ever tell the authorities what they knew. One of them would shortly be dead—and the other one would be wishing she were.

Lois Crane and Dora Phillips sat in numb silence, looking shocked by what they had just heard.

As Kemp rode away, Brubaugh closed the door, holding the ten thousand dollars in his hand.

"You gonna give us our cut now, Gavin?" Carl Blade asked.

"Not now," came the huge man's reply. "We need to make tracks. You'll each get your share, but only when Ma divides it up at the hideout. You know she always likes to do it that way." The gang leader stuffed the money back into its envelope, which he then slipped into his saddlebags. "Come on, boys. Let's get out of here. Tie up the women's hands again, and get 'em back on their horses."

Bill Kopack and Herman Tarver were huddled near Neal Shaffer's cot, and Brubaugh heard the low murmuring of their voices.

"Somethin' botherin' you two?" he grunted.

Tarver looked at his leader and said, "Gavin, Neal ain't in no shape to travel. Why don't we just hole up here for a few days and let him get to feelin' better?"

Brubaugh's heavy jaw jutted. "We're leavin' here now. We got to put as much distance as we can between us and Steamboat Springs—as fast as possible." His words were cold and carried a flat finality.

Walking stiffly toward Brubaugh, Kopack's face colored with anger, and stopping only inches from the man's large frame, he spat, "Neal can't travel, Gavin. He's still bleedin'. He'll die if we take him out of here now."

A fierce look settled in Brubaugh's wide-set eyes, and his thick lips became a tight, hard line. "A man that runs with this gang has got to be tough. If that was Ma Brubaugh layin' over there bleedin', she could still get up and ride a horse all day. If Neal's fit to run with us, he'll get back in his saddle."

Kopack bristled, but he was held in check when Shaffer said from his cot, "It's okay, Bill. I can do it."

Glaring hotly at Kopack, Brubaugh growled, "That takes care of it, don't it?"

"Look, Gavin," Carl Blade spoke up, "it's almost dark out there. Ain't no point in pressing on tonight. It's too dark, and there won't be no moon. If we can't get any farther, a posse can't either. Besides, those few stops we made to rest the horses weren't enough. They need to rest for the night."

Brubaugh strode over to the window and peered out. "Yeah, I guess you're right. Okay, we'll head out at first light. Bill, go get a few of them cans of beans out of my saddlebags. Here," he said, picking up a rusty, dented pot that was sitting on a shelf and handing it to Kopack, "start a fire out there and dump them beans in this thing. We may as well enjoy some hot food since it's too dark for anyone to spot our smoke."

Without waiting for a response, the huge man then looked at Carl Blade and said, "Carl, I've decided that we're takin' the young gal to the hideout. Ma will like her best. I'm assignin' you the job of disposin' of the other one. Be sure to hide the body good. We'll tie Lois up so's we can all get some sleep after we finish eatin'."

Dora Phillips felt as though her blood had turned to ice water. Her face blanched and her lips began quivering furiously as she tried to find her voice.

Lois Crane put her arms around the woman and spoke for her. "What are you talking about?" she demanded, staring in disbelief at the outlaw. "What kind of heartless beasts are you? You can't just kill Dora like she was a gnat or something! You cold-bloodedly murdered those men in town today for money, but in the name of heaven, nobody is paying you to kill Dora! You can't do this!"

Dora's voice was a mere squeak as she begged, "Please, Mr. Brubaugh, don't kill me! I haven't done anything to you!"

"Shut up!" barked the big man. "Carl, I told you what to do. You better get it done."

Lois bolted across the small room and stood in front of the huge outlaw, glaring at him. Her eyes were filled with both fear and fury, but the fury was stronger. "Haven't you an ounce of humanity in you?" she half screamed.

"I said she dies." His voice cut through Lois's fury like a knife.

Seeing that he was not about to change his mind, Lois swallowed hard and then said in a ragged, broken voice, "Then, please, Mr. Brubaugh . . . if . . . if somebody has to die, let it be me instead."

"Lois, no!" Dora cried, rising from her chair and stumbling toward her. Gripping Lois's shoulders, she sobbed, "There's no reason that it should be you instead of me."

Lois started to speak, but she was interrupted by Gavin Brubaugh, who said to her, "You'd really let me have you killed in place of this other one?"

"If only one of us could live, yes," replied Lois, lifting her chin defiantly.

Brubaugh's moods played close to the surface. He looked at the brunette, who stood little more than five feet tall, and said with admiration, "You're somethin' else, lady. I like a person with some grit in their craw—and you sure got grit. And because of that, you ain't to be the one that's gonna die. It's gonna be Dora, there."

Dora's weeping grew louder as she clung to Lois. Setting her jaw, the younger woman looked Brubaugh straight in the eye and said, "Neither one of us has to die. You can let us both go."

Brubaugh's mood went ugly again. "I can't let you go. I've got orders from Ma. One of you has to be taken to the hideout, and the other one has to be killed."

"Why did you take the two of us in the first place?"

"For hostages!" blurted the huge man. "Ma said to take two as a safety measure—and I do what Ma says. She said to kill the second one as soon as we was safe. I gotta do it!"

"What does she want the other one for? What is *my* purpose?"

"To be Ma's slave," came the direct answer. "You know—cleanin', washin', cookin', that kind of stuff."

"Well, then at least turn Dora loose and let her go. Your mother will never know the difference!"

Brubaugh suddenly looked extremely uncomfortable under Lois's hard glare. Shuffling his feet, he took a deep breath, then snapped back, "No way, lady. Nobody can fool Ma. She would know I was lyin'. I gotta kill Dora."

Lois was astounded that this huge monster of a man could be browbeaten and intimidated by a woman, even though she was his mother. Holding Dora in her arms,

Lois pressed Brubaugh further. "Look," she said, keeping a level tone, "two slaves would be better than one, wouldn't they? We're both young and healthy, and we're not strangers to hard work. We could please your mother twice as good. I'm sure she would agree if she saw us."

Lois watched her words take effect on the ugly giant as he slowly thought over what she had just said.

The gang members eyed each other, knowing how Ma Brubaugh was about being obeyed to the letter. Any deviation from her orders would bring down her wrath on the violator.

Standing there in the flickering yellow light of the single lantern, Brubaugh licked his thick lips and pondered the idea Lois had planted in his mind.

Carl Blade said, "Gavin, you'd better not give in to her. Your ma will have your hide."

Lois glared hotly at Blade and then said to Brubaugh, "Are you a puppet, or are you your own man? Show your mother you have a mind of your own—and can come up with your own good ideas. What I'm suggesting makes sense. Two women can surely do more work than one."

Fearful that Ma Brubaugh might take out her fury on all of them if her orders were disobeyed, Fred Foss shook his head in disagreement. "Gavin, we'd better kill this woman and get it over with."

Brubaugh's large nostrils flared with anger, and he snapped at Foss, "You shut up! And you, too, Carl. I say who lives and who dies here. I'm my own man, you know. Maybe I think it would be good to have two slaves at the hideout. Besides, Ma might really like the idea of havin' two women workin' for her. And if not, then Ma can give the order to kill Dora. Leastways, by my bringin' Dora in alive and tellin' Ma I thought up the idea, Ma'll know I got a mind of my own. She'll be proud that I done some good thinkin' by myself."

Daring them to disagree with either the idea or its origin, Brubaugh looked at each of his men in turn, staring them into submission.

The outlaws eyed each other with trepidation and then nodded to their leader. They were fearful of Ma's

reaction, but they feared her son as well. They said no
more and got ready to spend the night.

At dawn the next morning, the gang and their hostages struck out for northwestern Wyoming, toward the
wild Teton Forest.

They had traveled roughly twenty miles by noon,
when they stopped to rest beside a small creek. While the
men were watering the horses and filling their canteens,
Lois and Dora knelt beside the creek and washed their
hands and faces as best they could. After looking to see if
anyone was close enough to hear her, Lois whispered to
the older woman that she would make another attempt to
get her hands on a gun.

"Lois, no! It's far too dangerous," Dora cautioned.

"It seems to me that it's just as dangerous *not* to try
to escape. The future doesn't hold much promise for us
either way, does it?" the young woman reasoned.

The two women stood up, and Bill Kopack unexpect-
edly stepped up to them and put a grimy hand on Lois's
shoulder. "I'd still like to try on a kiss for size, little lady."

Giving him an icy look, Lois said, "Forget it, mister,"
and started to step around him.

But Kopack pulled her close to him, gripping the back
of her head with one hand and pressing his lips to hers.
When he finally released her, he looked deep into her eyes
and said, "That was pretty good, honey. How'd you like—?"

Lois cut off his words by digging her fingernails into
his cheekbones and raking them sharply down both sides
of his face. Howling in pain, he slapped her hard, sending
her to the ground with her head ringing.

Gavin Brubaugh saw what had happened and came
thundering over to Kopack. A low growl rumbled deep in
the giant's throat. Then he exploded, shouting, "What are
you doin' to that woman?"

Kopack touched his fingertips to the bleeding furrows
on his face and said, "Aw, I was just tryin' to be friendly."

Scrambling to her feet, Lois snarled through bared
teeth, "He put his filthy mouth on mine. Tell him to leave
me alone!"

Pointing a stiff finger in Kopack's face, the beefy man blared, "Bill, keep your paws off her, you hear me?"

Kopack's temper ignited. "You don't own me, Brubaugh." He spat. "If I want to be friendly with a woman, it's none of your business."

Brubaugh was amazingly fast for a man of his weight. He unleashed his right fist like a steel piston, and it struck Kopack's jaw solidly, lifting the gang member off his feet and flopping him hard to the ground, flat on his back. Rolling his head twice, he then went unconscious.

Brubaugh turned around to Lois. "These boys get a little out of hand once in a while, lady. I don't think he'll bother you again."

Clinging to the younger woman, Dora looked up at the giant piteously and said in a trembling voice, "Please, Mr. Brubaugh, won't you just let us go?"

Brubaugh frowned, his mood changing again. "Can't do that, lady. Don't ask me no more."

Saying nothing, the other men gathered around Bill Kopack as he began to stir. He seemed to have a hard time coming to. Eager to get moving toward the hideout, Brubaugh bent over and picked him up by the belt and shirt. Then he carried him to the creek and plunged his head into the cold water. Kopack's body jerked, and his head came up. He coughed, choked, coughed again, and swore.

Brubaugh dropped him on the bank and then stood over him like a giant tree until he was sure Kopack was able to see him clearly. "Don't you ever mouth off to me again, Bill," he warned. "Next time I'll knock that stupid head of yours clean off. And you stay away from those women. I ain't tellin' you again. Now let's get movin'."

Bill Kopack rolled to his knees, shaking his head, and then stood up. Rubbing his aching jaw, he winced as his hand touched the raw furrows that Lois had plowed on his cheeks. He got to his feet and silently made his way to Neal Shaffer to help the wounded man back on his horse.

The gang had traveled another three hours, still on a beeline for northwestern Wyoming, when, as they were pulling up out of a draw, Neal Shaffer suddenly slipped from his saddle and sprawled on the ground. Bill Kopack quickly dismounted and knelt at Shaffer's side while the others remained on their mounts.

Kopack looked up at Herman Tarver and said, "Herm, give me a hand. He needs some water."

Tarver dismounted and lifted Shaffer's canteen from his saddlehorn. Shaffer looked up at Kopack with dull eyes and said, "Bill . . . I can't . . . go any farther."

Kopack put the canteen to Shaffer's lips, looking up at Gavin Brubaugh, who was still astride his horse. "Neal says he can't continue. You all go ahead. I'll stay here with him till he's able to ride. We'll catch up with you."

"Can't do that," Brubaugh said coldly.

"What do you mean you can't do that?" said Kopack stiffly. "What's to keep you? Go on. I'll take care of Neal."

Swinging his thick leg over the saddle and easing to the ground to the sound of squeaking leather, Brubaugh walked to where Shaffer lay and said, "You're not thinkin', Bill. We shot Colorado's governor full of lead yesterday. Do you think the authorities are gonna take that lightly? The government's gonna have somebody on our tails at any time now. The only safe place for any of us to be is the hideout."

"If I ain't worried about it," argued Kopack, who remained on his knees, "why should you be? I told you to go on to the hideout. Only Neal and me would have anything to worry about."

"Like I said," grunted the huge man, "you ain't thinkin'. If the law catches up to you, they'll force you to tell where the hideout is."

Disgust showed in Kopack's eyes. "Gavin, I've ridden with you for six years. You know I ain't gonna tell no lawmen where the hideout is. Now get on outta here. Neal and I will be along when he's able."

Without another word, Brubaugh pulled his gun and cocked the hammer. Before anyone could say or do anything, he pointed the muzzle at Shaffer's head and, completely emotionless, fired. The gun bucked in his hand, the report echoing across the Wyoming hills.

There was murder in Bill Kopack's eyes, but it vanished quickly as Brubaugh thumbed back the hammer again and aimed the smoking weapon at the bridge of the man's nose. "Were you gonna say somethin', Bill?"

Kopack stood up, and Brubaugh followed his nose with the barrel of his revolver. Holding it steady, he waited for a response.

Kopack blinked and said in a low voice, "No. I wasn't gonna say anything."

"Good." Brubaugh grinned, blowing the smoke from the muzzle. "Now the problem is solved, and as soon as you throw Shaffer's carcass over there in that ditch, we can keep on ridin'." Gavin Brubaugh wheeled and started for his horse, holstering his gun.

Hatred suddenly welled up in Bill Kopack like some living, deadly thing. He whipped out the nine-inch hunting knife that he wore in a sheath on his belt and charged after the huge man with his teeth clenched, berserk with fury.

Fred Foss called out, "Gavin! Behind you!"

Brubaugh pivoted just in time to dodge the blade. His huge, strong hand gripped Kopack's wrist, twisting it. The bone popped, and the knife fell to the ground from Kopack's now-useless fingers.

Descending on the smaller man like a massive grizzly, Brubaugh seized hold of him and whirled him around. Then he ran both hands up under Kopack's armpits and laced his fingers together at the back of his neck while Kopack gritted his teeth and tried desperately to break the hold. But the gang leader's strength was too much for him.

"Stab me in the back, will you?" roared Brubaugh. While the women quaked in terror and the other gang members watched in awe, the powerful giant lifted Kopack off the ground, then with a breathy grunt brought his interlaced hands together with all his strength.

Bill Kopack's spine snapped violently, and his body went limp.

Breathing heavily, more from anger than exertion, Brubaugh let Kopack's lifeless form slide to the ground.

Dora Phillips felt nauseated. Still in the saddle, she laid her head over her wrists, which were tied to the pommel, and she tried not to vomit.

Lois Crane stared at Brubaugh in disbelief. If he had to kill the man, why did he have to do it in such a hideous and brutal manner? Wouldn't a bullet have been faster and more humane? *But then*, she asked herself, *what do these savages care about being humane?*

Gavin Brubaugh and his three remaining men disposed of the two bodies by stuffing them in a thicket at the bottom of the gully. Then they pushed on. Blade, Tarver, and Foss were riled by the killing of their cronies, but Brubaugh soothed them by reminding them that their share of the money would now be larger, and he promised Foss an extra bonus for warning him about Kopack's attempt at stabbing him in the back.

Lois stole a glance at Dora. She tried not to let her fear show on her face, but she was fast coming to the terrible conclusion that escape would not be possible—and that their situation was hopeless.

It was late morning the following day when the procession rode around a large butte and came upon two young Indians. One of them was pinned under a dead horse while the other was trying vainly to get the animal off his friend.

"Looks like they've got trouble, Gavin," Fred Foss said.

"I'd say so," the outlaw leader responded gleefully, his hatred of Indians coming to the surface. "Ain't that just too bad."

Pulling her mount alongside Brubaugh, Lois Crane said, "You *will* stop and help him, won't you?"

The outlaw chuckled. "Sure, lady. I'll help him."

Blade, Tarver, and Foss gave each other knowing glances as the outlaw led them and their hostages up to the young Indians. Then Brubaugh turned to his men. "Okay, boys, let's get down."

While the men were dismounting, the young Indian who was attempting to free his friend straightened up, dusted off his buckskins, and smiled at them.

"What happened?" asked Brubaugh.

"My companion cannot move," the Indian responded. "His pony stepped into a hole, and the animal went down and fell on top of Tall Tree. I shot the pony to relieve it of its misery."

Brubaugh knew that these young braves were Shoshone. "What're you two doin' here, anyway? I thought all you people were placed on the Wind River Reservation farther east and were told to stay there."

The young brave squared his shoulders and stared unwaveringly at Gavin Brubaugh. "This land belongs to Ute, Sioux, Shoshone, and Blackfoot. White man have no right to put us on a reservation. We ride with Chief Iron Jaw."

Brubaugh and his men looked at each other. They knew that Chief Iron Jaw was the leader of a band of Shoshone renegades. The young chief had refused to stay on the reservation, and the army had not been able to run him down and capture him. They also knew that the fierce Iron Jaw had no love for white men.

"My name is Red Feather," continued the young brave. "I wish you no harm. I ask as one man of other men, will you help me free Tall Tree from his horse?"

Looking down at the other Indian, whose body was held firm by the weight of the dead horse, Brubaugh pulled his gun and squinted at Red Feather. "If a bullet was good enough for the pinto, why ain't it good enough for your friend?"

As Red Feather looked at Brubaugh with disbelief, Herman Tarver quickly sidled up to the gang leader. "Gavin," he gasped, "it wouldn't be smart to do anything rash here. You know how them Indians can track a man. Iron Jaw would be on our tails for sure."

"Indians shouldn't be left alive," mumbled Brubaugh. "Like rattlesnakes, you gotta kill every one of 'em you see."

Red Feather was frozen, his eyes wide.

"Gavin, Herm's right," Carl Blade chimed in. "We don't need the likes of Iron Jaw to contend with. Let's help the kid out from under the horse and be on our way."

"I'd rather shoot him."

Red Feather suddenly wheeled and bolted for his pinto, and he was on its back almost before Brubaugh realized what was happening. Raising his gun, the outlaw snapped back the hammer and fired. The Indian jerked from the impact of the bullet but stayed on the back of the galloping horse, and within seconds he was out of sight.

"I'd better go after him!" gasped Tarver.

"Forget him," said Brubaugh, cocking his gun again. He aimed the gun at Tall Tree and casually shot him through the head as the others looked on, aghast. The two women screamed with fear and revulsion.

Holstering the smoking gun, Brubaugh grunted, "Now we can ride on."

Fred Foss stepped in front of the huge man and said sharply, "Gavin, you know I usually go along with just about anything you do, but that was downright stupid! This is gonna bring Iron Jaw right down on our necks!"

Brubaugh stared at the man for several moments. "I'm gonna hold back my temper for you talkin' to me so disrespectful-like, Fred, 'cause I'm still feelin' kindly for your keepin' Kopack from stabbin' me in the back." Breaking open his gun to reload it, he admitted, "Sometimes my dislike for redskins makes me act first and think later, but what's done is done. The only thing we can do now is cover our trail real careful-like. I'll just have to outsmart that stinkin' Iron Jaw."

Blade, Tarver, and Foss felt sick as they returned to their horses. Despite his bravado, they knew there was no way the likes of Gavin Brubaugh could outsmart the resourceful and virulent Shoshone chief.

Chapter Four

A cool north wind swirled up the dusty street against the citizens, horses, and buildings of Rock Springs as the brilliant sun started its climb into the flawless Wyoming sky.

Western Union telegrapher Wally Teeters unlocked his office and closed the door behind him, wiping his left eye to remove a piece of grit thrown up by the wind. He slipped out of his wool jacket, hung it on a wall peg, and then placed his hat over it. He was settling his green visor on his head when the telegraph receiver began to click.

Dashing over to his desk, the middle-aged man quickly picked up a pencil. The message was a lengthy one, and as he carefully wrote down every letter, he kept raising his bushy brown eyebrows and shaking his head at its contents.

When the message was completed, Teeters jumped up and removed his visor, clapped his hat back on, and threw on his jacket. Not bothering to button it, he hurried out the door and up the street toward the Frontier Hotel, his head bent against the wind.

Bursting through the door of the hotel, Teeters dashed across the lobby to the desk and demanded of the desk clerk, "Ray, which room is Marshal Day staying in?"

"Room five," the clerk replied. "But he's not in right now. Glenn came in for him earlier, and they went over to the Bluebell to have breakfast."

"Good, that's even better," the telegrapher said. "The marshal won't have to go looking for his deputy."

Running the few doors down the street to the Bluebell Café, Wally Teeters dashed into the restaurant and looked around the crowded room. He spotted U.S. Marshal Patrick Day and his deputy, Glenn Childress, at a table near the front window. Teeters weaved his way among the tables and drew up to the two sandy-haired lawmen, idly thinking that they looked remarkably alike, even though thirty-eight-year-old Patrick Day was of medium build and stood five feet ten while his deputy, who had just turned twenty-five, was quite slender and stood an even six feet in height.

A bit short of breath, the telegrapher said, "Good mornin', Marshal. Deputy Childress."

"Morning, Wally," the marshal and his deputy said simultaneously.

"Marshal," said the telegrapher, "this telegram just came in for you. I figured it's very important, so I thought I'd run it over to you immediately."

"That was good of you, Wally," Day said, accepting the two-page telegram. "Care to join us?"

"No, I've got to get back to my office. But thanks for the offer, Marshal." Teeters turned and made an exit as quick as his entry had been.

Glenn Childress, taking a mouthful of his scrambled eggs, waited patiently while his superior read the lengthy message. He could tell by the look on Day's face that the news was not good.

When the marshal had finished reading, he looked intently at Childress and said glumly, "It's from Bill Kettering in Denver. You've heard of the Bess Brubaugh gang?"

"Yeah. Who hasn't? They call her Ma Brubaugh."

"Kettering's been informed that Ma Brubaugh's son Gavin and five of their men assassinated Colorado's governor, Roger Whitson, in Steamboat Springs yesterday, where Whitson had made a stop on his whistle-stop tour. The gang shot him while he was giving a speech. They also killed the county sheriff and his deputy, and the governor's two bodyguards. A number of bystanders were severely wounded, as well."

Shaking his head, Childress unleashed a low whistle and an oath.

"There's more," Day continued. "Brubaugh and his bloody bunch also kidnapped two women. It's presumed that the gang's headed for northwestern Wyoming. Kettering says it's believed that Ma Brubaugh and her cutthroats are maintaining a hideout somewhere deep in the Teton Forest. And *that* means her son's route had to lead them pretty close to Rock Springs, so even though they've been riding hard since yesterday, we'll have barely lost any time in catching up with them."

"It looks like you and I have a new assignment," said the deputy, setting down his coffee cup.

Day nodded. "Kettering wants us on their trail ten minutes ago. He mentions here that a posse out of Steamboat Springs was hot on Gavin Brubaugh's trail but failed to catch him and his men by the time they crossed the border into Wyoming. The task is ours alone now."

"I've heard that the Ma Brubaugh gang is a pretty big bunch."

"I think she usually keeps about eight or ten men, plus herself and her two sons."

"We'll need help once we locate them," said Childress. "Some local lawmen, I presume?"

"The trouble is there aren't too many lawmen north of here," responded Day. "We might just have to enlist help from the citizenry in the small towns and villages. The main thing now is to get going immediately. If we can spot their trail quick and ride hard, we might be able to catch up with Brubaugh and his bunch before they reach the hideout. The odds will be in our favor if we can take them before they've joined their other forces there."

Deputy Childress took a final sip of his coffee and said, "I've heard that Ma Brubaugh is a tough old girl."

"Like boot leather." Day nodded. "Bitter and heartless, with ice in her veins. Vigilantes hanged her oldest son for murder and horse stealing about nine years ago. When her husband wouldn't do anything about getting revenge, she split his head open with an ax and took up the task herself. Within a month's time, she'd killed every

one of the vigilantes personally—two of them with her
bare hands, or so rumor has it. No one could ever prove
anything. She and her remaining two boys have been on
the outlaw trail ever since. Well, then," the marshal said,
wiping his mouth with his napkin and standing up, "let's
get cracking."

Half a day after riding out of Rock Springs at a gallop,
the two federal lawmen managed to find the trail of the
Brubaugh gang, thankful that the weather had cooperated.
Had it rained, the lawmen would have had no clues to
follow.

Reading the undisturbed sign at a trot, they followed
the tracks down into a gully, whose floor was thick with
brush and small trees. Day and Childress halted their
mounts near a heavy stand of brush where the gang had
apparently stopped and dismounted.

Climbing down from their saddles, they began to
inspect the area. A small flock of blackbirds, their wings
whirring, took off from the thicket as the two men walked
along the edge of the brush, following boot tracks.

"Look at the depth of those prints," Day said to his
boss. "They carried something back in here, and I want to
know what it is."

Seconds later, Childress pointed into the thicket and
said, "Dead men, Pat. That's what they were carrying."

The lawmen dragged the bodies of Neal Shaffer and
Bill Kopack from the thicket into the open sunlight. Day
figured the two men had been dead for almost twenty-four
hours. There was no identification on either corpse.

Standing over them, the marshal said, "I'd lay my last
dollar that these two were part of the gang. It looks like
this one with the bullet in his head had become a burden.
See there? That wound in his side was pretty bad. Brubaugh
probably decided he was slowing them down too much."

Bending down over Bill Kopack, Childress said, "No
bullets in this one, but he got himself a broken neck
somehow."

"He probably also tangled with Brubaugh," mused

Day. "He and his ma both like to use their brute strength to kill and maim."

Glenn Childress lifted his hat and scratched his head. "Is the other son the same way?"

"Not as much," replied the marshal. "I understand he's a bit slow-minded—a little molasses stuck in his brain. He's also the youngest, and the way I hear it, because he's slow, the old woman babies him a lot. He's as big as a house, like his mother and brother, but he only gets dangerous if he's riled. Ma and Gavin, on the other hand, are dangerous even when they're asleep."

Tugging his hat back squarely onto his head, Childress said, "Well, at least with these two out of the picture, the odds are better for us."

"Can't argue with that," the marshal said. "Well, let's move on. We'll just have to leave these boys for the bugs and the critters. No time to bury them."

The federal men pressed onward. It was early afternoon the next day when they saw three buzzards circling lazily overhead in the azure sky.

Childress pointed at them and said, "They're investigating something just up ahead. You don't suppose we're going to find another dead gang member?"

"We'll know in a few minutes," said Day. "Whatever it is that those buzzards have spotted is directly in front of us. Just the other side of that butte, I'd say."

Ten minutes later, Day and Childress saw the dead pinto, its foreleg still caught deep in a gopher hole. They were surprised when they saw the lifeless form of a young Indian pinned beneath the horse. Drawing close, the lawmen dismounted and examined the Indian's body.

"Shot in the head just like that outlaw," Day said disgustedly. Looking around, he declared, "These tracks were definitely made by Brubaugh and his gang. Looks like he and his pals stopped right here and found this kid trapped by his horse. Looks like they shot the kid rather than help him get free."

Noticing a bullet hole in the pinto's head, Childress

was puzzled. "Pat, do you think Brubaugh or one of his cronies would have had the compassion to shoot this pony?"

"I doubt it," came the marshal's reply.

"Well, it's a cinch this Indian didn't put the slug in its head. The angle's all wrong."

Making a circle, the lawmen soon found the tracks of Red Feather's unshod horse leading away from the scene. It was easy to tell that it had left at a gallop.

"I wonder what this kid was doing off the reservation," Childress said.

"I don't know, but he sure learned the hard way that with hatred still running high around here, leaving the reservation can be mighty dangerous." He sighed and shook his head. "Come on. I'm afraid we don't have any time to bury this poor devil, either."

Riding on, they found that the gang's trail was more difficult to follow, as if Gavin Brubaugh had suddenly decided to cover his tracks.

It was midafternoon when Gavin Brubaugh reined in his mount at the top of a ridge so that it and the other horses could be rested. Everyone dismounted, and the two hostages were allowed to go off a ways to refresh themselves. Returning to where the others were, Lois Crane and Dora Phillips sat down on the ground against a fir tree, aware that the country was becoming increasingly rugged and cooler as they drew nearer to the Teton Forest.

Herman Tarver had tethered the horses alongside a small trickling brook, and while the horses drank, he decided to climb up a tall boulder and take a look around. The broad sweep of land stretched for miles before him, and shading his eyes against the bright sun, he carefully scanned the trail they had ridden, at the same time listening to the conversation that was going on ten feet below him between Brubaugh and the other men.

Gavin Brubaugh was saying to Carl Blade and Fred Foss, "We'll be at the hideout by tomorrow mornin', boys. Now, we gotta keep Ma from knowin' about our meetin' up with them Indians."

"You mean you don't want her findin' out you killed one of 'em and wounded the other?" asked Foss.

"Yeah, that's exactly what I mean," snarled Brubaugh. "She'd just about cut me in half for doin' somethin' so dumb, so you guys make sure you don't say nothin' about it, understand?"

"Yeah," said Foss as he and Blade both nodded.

Brubaugh lifted his gaze to Tarver up on the rock and said, "You hear that, Herm?"

"Yeah, Gavin," Tarver replied. "I ain't gonna say nothin'."

Turning to the two women, who were still huddled against the huge fir tree, the outlaw said stiffly, "You two ladies better not say anything about it, either."

"We won't," Lois assured him, looking at Dora.

"Gavin!" Herman Tarver suddenly hissed from atop the rock.

"What is it?" Brubaugh looked up at him, worry creasing his narrow forehead. "Don't tell me Iron Jaw's comin'!"

"No, but it's two white men, and they're headin' straight for us. They're ridin' slow, and they keep stoppin' and studyin' the ground. They're followin' our trail, sure as shootin'."

Gavin Brubaugh swung a meaty fist through the air and cursed. "I knew the law would be on us," he spat. "I just didn't think they'd find us this fast. How close are they, Herm?"

"A couple of miles. At the rate they're movin', it'll probably take 'em half an hour or better to get here."

"Good!" the huge man said with a wicked grin. "That'll give us time to set a trap."

Calling Tarver down, Brubaugh scrutinized the area and decided to ambush the two lawmen from behind the rock. He gave orders for the women to be bound and gagged and hidden farther down the trail with the horses. Then the four men waited, taking their places in clefts of the rock.

In the stillness of the morning air, Brubaugh gathered the other men around him and said, "I been thinkin'.

Maybe we ought to take one of these badge toters alive in case other lawmen show up later. You know how they stick together—sort of a brotherhood. With a live one, we'd have some bargaining power if others showed up."

"I don't know, Gavin," said Carl Blade. "That means we'd have to watch him all the time."

"We can tie him up," countered Brubaugh. "I think Ma would want me to bring one of 'em in. If she doesn't see it that way, we can always kill him later." He shifted in his place. "When they come into view, I'll tell you which one we'll kill, and we'll all hit him at once. I'll handle takin' the other one alive."

U.S. Marshal Patrick Day and Deputy U.S. Marshal Glenn Childress leaned over in their saddles as they kept their steady pace toward the northwest, continually studying the ground for sign of the Brubaugh gang and their hostages.

"They're usin' branches, all right," said Childress. "They do a pretty good job of covering the tracks, but the effort's costing them some time. The tracks are very fresh. We've definitely gained on them."

"Looks like it," said Day. "We'd better be more cautious. If they should spot us, they might try an ambush."

"You're the man of experience," the deputy said with a smile. "I'm sure you know how outlaws think better than I do."

"Once we know for certain where they are," said Day, "the best thing for us to do is circle around in front of them. The two of us ought to be able to capture four unsuspecting men."

"Maybe more," Childress added. "There are six horses, after all, and we're not positive that the women are riding singly."

The marshal's line of sight was drawn to a tall rock about thirty yards away that towered over the ridge. Suddenly he drew in on the reins.

Childress halted his mount as well and asked, "What's the matter?"

Staring at the rock, the marshal replied, "I'm not

sure, but I think I saw the glint of sunlight on something metallic. Might be a gun barrel. We'd better—"

Day's words were cut short by a barrage of gunfire from the shadowed clefts of the rock. Glenn Childress was knocked from his horse in a hail of hot lead.

Day dived from his horse's back, hit the ground, and frantically looked around for cover. Expecting the ambushers to unleash their weapons on him, he whipped out his gun and started running back down the trail.

Instead, a deep gravelly voice shouted, "Hold it right there, or you're a dead man!"

Knowing the ambushers had his back in their gunsights, Day stopped short and threw his hands in the air. He could hear footsteps behind him, and then the same voice bellowed, "Drop the gun!"

The marshal let the revolver slip from his fingers and drop to the ground. Then he turned around. Four men were coming toward him, their guns ready. He knew who the leader was by the man's size.

Gavin Brubaugh halted a few feet from the marshal as the others drew up beside him. The outlaw looked at the badge on Day's chest and said, "We got us a real genuine United States marshal, boys. What's your name, lawman?"

"Patrick Day," came the steady answer.

Carl Blade, who had stopped to check on Glenn Childress, lying in a crumpled heap on the ground, came up behind the thick-bodied giant. "The other one's dead, Gavin."

An evil grin spread over Brubaugh's face as he kept his eyes on Day and said, " 'Course he is. Ain't nothin' could live through that much firepower. But, now, this one . . . this one's goin' home with us."

"What are you planning?" the marshal asked.

"Gonna use you for a little insurance," replied Brubaugh. "I figure when you and your dead pal back there turn up missin', there'll no doubt be more just like you comin' after us. But they ain't gonna kill us if they gotta go through you to do so." Over his shoulder, he said, "Check his saddlebags, boys. You'll find a pair of handcuffs

in there, I reckon. May as well put them to good use,
don't you agree, Marshal?" Brubaugh said with a sneer.
Speaking to his men, he added, "Then get him up on his
horse, nice and gentle-like. We wouldn't want to hurt our
valuable property."

The three men dumped the body of Glenn Childress
in a nearby crevice, and then they brought the women
out. Despite the marshal's also being a hostage, Dora and
Lois were glad to see that he had been spared. Even
though he was as helpless as they were, they had a better
chance of escape with him alive.

The procession forged ahead, with the deputy's rider-
less horse trailing behind. Patrick Day mourned the loss of
his friend, but he kept his mind from dwelling on Childress's
murder by trying to figure out how he could free the two
women and himself from the hands of the heartless outlaws.

Two days passed before they reached the outskirts of
the Teton Forest. To the northwest, beyond rolling mead-
ows of grass dotted with scarlet gilia and goldenrod, were
jagged mountain ridges fringed by dark green and blue
conifers, along with white-barked birch and aspen.

Passing by the western shore of New Fork Lake, they
entered the broad valley between Hoback Peak and Fre-
mont Peak, whose majestic heads stood well over ten
thousand feet above sea level. Toward sundown, they
were deep in the forest on the west side of the Wind River
Range, roughly forty miles southeast of Jackson. Through
the tall lodgepole pines, they saw the lofty snowcapped
top of Gannett Peak catch the fire of the setting sun.

Gavin Brubaugh called for them to quicken their
pace. "We've only got about ten miles to go, and I don't
cotton to spendin' another night on the trail. You women,
spur them horses."

Looking at the federal marshal, who was handcuffed
and tied securely to the saddle, he sneered. "Lawman, do
you realize how concerned we are about your safety? See,
we didn't tie you to your saddle because we thought you'd
escape—we was afraid you'd fall off!" The big man guffawed at his joke, and his gang members all joined in.

With Brubaugh in the lead, the gang members and the three hostages threaded their way among the dense trees through the dappled sunlight. After traveling for just over an hour, they crossed a wide meadow. On the far end of it the forest began again, and as they rode through the trees, they came to a small clearing, bordered by a creek. There stood a large log cabin with a privy twenty feet behind it. On the front porch sat three men, smoking cigarettes.

The men stood up when they saw the procession enter the clearing. One of them, a bulky overall-clad hulk who strongly resembled Gavin Brubaugh, dashed inside the house, shouting, "Ma, Gavin's back! Gavin's back, Ma!"

The two other men, both of average height and weight and in their midthirties, stepped off the porch and eyed the newcomers.

"Howdy, R. W., Art. Where's Ma?" Gavin Brubaugh asked.

"Hecky went to get her," R. W. Moffitt answered.

"Gavin, where's Bill and Neal? Did you kill the governor? How come—"

Brubaugh interrupted Art Wilson's questions. "You'll learn it all while I tell Ma about it." Turning to his fellow travelers, he said, "All right, everybody. Out of your saddles. This is the end of the line. R. W., help that lawman off his horse—and keep your hands off them women!"

Hecky Brubaugh lumbered out of the cabin and approached the riders. The twenty-one-year-old man had the same homely features, the same hairline, and the same heft as his older brother; however, Hecky's mouth hung loosely, and there was a slight dullness to his eyes.

"Ma will be out in a minute, Gavin," he said excitedly to his brother.

As Dora and Lois started dismounting, Hecky spotted them, and grinning broadly, he said, "Hey, Gavin, where'd you get the girls?"

Hecky moved toward the women, licking his lips appreciatively. He eyed them both and then stepped close to Lois, who had thrown her right leg over the pommel and was tugging at her skirt. Looking up at her, his yellow teeth showing in his wide smile, he raised his hands toward her and said, "Here, girl, I'll help you down."

Lois shuddered at the thought of this filthy oaf touching her, but since he was standing in her way, she did not have any choice. She managed to conceal her distaste and leaned toward him. Hecky's powerful arms lowered her to the ground as if she weighed no more than the clothing on her body.

Releasing her when her feet touched the ground, the man grinned and said, "My name's Hecky. What's yours?"

Lois, feeling a touch of pity for the slow-minded young man and appreciating the kindness he had shown her, tried to ignore the foulness of his breath. But his size and strength frightened her. Taking a step backward, she forced a smile and said, "My name is Lois, Hecky. I . . . I'm glad to meet you."

Tilting his head sideways, Hecky said, "You sure are pretty, Lois. I like you."

"Thank you, Hecky," the brunette replied weakly as Dora sidled up to her, fear creasing the older woman's face.

Everyone turned at the sudden heavy footsteps pounding through the door of the cabin. Bess Brubaugh—known far and wide as Ma Brubaugh—emerged and stood there, hands on her hips and scowling. She was a stout, powerful woman, in height and breadth more like a man. Five feet ten and weighing two hundred and seventy pounds, she had graying hair that was chopped short and severe like a man's, and the clothing she wore—wool shirt, bib overalls, and heavy work boots—furthered her masculine image. Her left leg had a pronounced limp, the result of her having been gored by a bull almost thirty years before.

At fifty-five, Ma's deeply lined face looked like shoe leather, and though it was round and fleshy, there was a cruel, hard line to it. Anyone looking at her sons would see where they got their low hairlines, thick, bushy eyebrows, wide-set pale blue eyes, and broad noses.

She dropped her arms and stepped off the porch into

the sunlight, ignoring the smoke from the cigarette that dangled from the corner of her sour-looking mouth. Glaring at the two women and the lawman, she limped toward her elder son and the men he had taken on the mission. She looked sharply at Gavin, and the others braced themselves for the inevitable explosion.

Before Ma could speak, Brubaugh hurried to her, smiling broadly, and placed the large brown envelope in her hands.

"We did it, Ma!" he quickly said with elation. "There's the ten thousand dollars to prove it. Roger Whitson is dead, and Bart Kemp is happy. He said to tell you that your plan was thought out real good, and that me and the boys carried it off perfect."

Opening the envelope and running her fat thumb over the edge of the bills, she mumbled, "You count it?"

"Sure did, Ma. It's all there."

Taking a deep pull on the cigarette, Ma Brubaugh ran her stern eyes over the faces of the group, staring again at the two women and the marshal. "Where are Bill and Neal?" she demanded of Brubaugh.

Stammering somewhat at first, Gavin Brubaugh told his mother how Neal Shaffer had taken a bullet in the gunfight at the Steamboat Springs depot. Bending the truth slightly to make himself look good, his voice grew more confident as he explained that Shaffer could not continue and that Bill Kopack had turned on him. Brubaugh was careful not to mention killing the Shoshone and wounding his friend, who had escaped.

Ma listened with cold, silent patience as her son reeled off his story. "So you see, Ma," he concluded, "I had to kill 'em both. You'd have done it if you'd been there." Looking to Blade, Tarver, and Foss for support, he added, "Wouldn't she, fellas?"

"Sure would," spoke up Fred Foss, knowing it was to his advantage to side with Brubaugh. "Like he said, Ma, Bill was gonna stab him in the back—I was the one who called out to warn him—so Gavin didn't have no choice. And Gavin's right. He couldn't leave Shaffer and Kopack out there for lawmen to pick 'em up and force 'em to tell where the hideout is."

"Yeah, and lawmen showed up just like I figured they would, Ma," Brubaugh added. "We killed the partner of this one."

Ma Brubaugh looked U.S. Marshal Patrick Day up and down with disgust. Then she turned back to her son. "So what's he doin' still breathin'? How come you took him with you and didn't kill him?"

"Well, Ma," Brubaugh replied, running a shaky hand over his mouth, "I figure when the two lawmen don't show up back wherever they came from, there's gonna be more comin' to look for 'em. After all, we did kill Colorado's governor, you know. So I did my own thinkin'. I figured if this one was still alive when the others showed up, we'd have 'em by the nose. They'd be scared to come in and try to take us 'cause we'd have one of their own— and we'd kill him if they try anything." Smiling proudly and hooking his thumbs in his overall straps, he said, "How's that for good thinkin', Ma?"

Without comment, the big woman gestured at her men and said gruffly, "Take the stinkin' lawman and tie him to one of them posts on the porch."

Marshal Day finally spoke up. "Mrs. Brubaugh, I think you'd best consider what you're doing. I'm a United States marshal. By holding me, you are inviting the federal government to come down on your head."

"Shut up!" Ma snarled. Then she turned her attention to the two women. They stood frozen with fear as she limped toward them.

From behind her, Brubaugh quickly said, "Ma, let me explain—"

Ma stopped and looked over her shoulder at her elder son with angry eyes. Flicking the stub of her cigarette to the ground and stepping on it, she snarled, "I'll deal with you in a minute!" Then looking the women over with a deep scowl on her homely face, she said to the redhead, "What's your name?"

Swallowing hard, Dora answered, "Dora Phillips."

"And you?" Ma said to the brunette.

"My name is Lois Crane," came the firm reply, "and I think you should listen to the marshal and release the three of us."

"Nobody around here cares what you think, girl!" snapped the old woman. Pivoting, she glared at Brubaugh and screamed, "I want to know why you brung two women! I told you to kill the other one!"

Brubaugh shambled over to her and said, "Ma, I thought havin' two slaves would be better than one. I thought—"

Ma's right hand lashed out, savagely stinging Brubaugh's cheek with her open palm. Eyes blazing with fury, she bellowed, "You don't do the thinkin' around here. I do! Understand?" She slapped him again, only harder. "I don't want you thinkin'! I want you obeyin'!" Then she hit her son a third time.

Brubaugh's hand went to his burning cheek as Ma turned around and limped back to the porch. His narrowed eyes followed his mother, revealing a hatred boiling within him, but he said nothing.

After Ma had checked the handcuffs around the marshal's wrists, she opened the brown envelope and gave five hundred dollars to each gang member as his share of the assassination money. She stuffed the rest of the money in her bib pocket to keep for herself.

Brubaugh walked over to the porch and said in a hurt tone, "I want my share, Ma."

Regarding her son with disgust, the old woman spat. "You'll get your share when you take the redhead out into the woods and come back without her!"

Rubbing the back of his hand against his welted cheek, Brubaugh wheeled and headed toward Dora, who began to weep loudly.

Suddenly Hecky called out, "Wait a minute, Ma. Why not make Dora do the work and let Lois be my girl? I really like her!"

Ma Brubaugh was touched by the pitiful look in her favorite son's eyes. Hecky's doglike devotion to his mother endeared him to her, and she denied him little.

Pressing the issue, Hecky grinned and said, "It'd make me real happy, Ma."

As she silently studied Hecky's face, tenderness softened her hard countenance. "All right, honey. If it'll make you happy. But Lois will have to work, too."

Hecky's thick lips split into a broad grin, exposing his yellow teeth, as he looked at Lois. "If you can be my girl, you won't mind doin' some work, will you, Lois?"

The pretty brunette heard Dora release a tremulous sigh of relief, and she was glad that the numb-minded oaf had talked his mother into sparing Dora's life, but she cringed at the horrid thought of becoming Hecky's property. She felt sick all over as she responded weakly, "No, Hecky. I won't mind doing some work."

Gavin Brubaugh stepped over to his mother. "I guess that means I can have my share of the money, right, Ma?"

Giving her son a sour look, she said, "Yeah, you can have your share. But if you disobey my orders again, I'm takin' it back. Understand?"

Leaving the men outside, Ma Brubaugh roughly shoved Dora and Lois into the cabin, where she explained to them what their duties would be. "If you don't do everything I tell you, you'll feel the bite of my whip. And you," she said to Lois, "even though you're now Hecky's woman, that don't mean you don't have to do your share of the chores. If you fail in any way, you're gonna face my wrath." She squinted her eyes at the two shaking women and warned, "If either one of you even tries to escape, both of you will be killed immediately. You got that?"

Lois and Dora nodded numbly, eyeing each other with hopelessness.

More than a week passed, and as each day went by with no sign of Iron Jaw, Gavin Brubaugh breathed a little easier. No one had uttered a word about the incident with the Indians, and it was all but forgotten.

Ma sent Carl Blade into Jackson, thirty miles west of the hideout, for supplies. When he returned the next day, he told the gang that he had good news.

"When I was in town, I heard that a Wells Fargo

stage from Denver is due to arrive tomorrow, around six. There's a new bank opening, and the stage will be carrying money fresh from the Denver mint for its first day of business."

Gathering the men together, Ma ordered Gavin Brubaugh to choose three men to take with him the next morning. They would ride to the new bridge that crossed over the Snake River five miles south of Jackson, and there they would hold up the incoming stage.

Brubaugh thought carefully, then chose Fred Foss, along with Art Wilson and R. W. Moffitt, who had stayed behind during the assassination of the governor. "We'll have us some fun, boys," the huge man said gleefully, clapping each of them on the shoulder as he strode outside and sat on the front porch to enjoy the sight of the U.S. marshal languishing against the post.

Hecky came out and unlocked the handcuffs while Carl Blade kept his gun trained on the lawman. "Time for you to hit the privy," the slow-witted young man declared. "Then my girl, Lois, has some chow for you."

The marshal said nothing, battling his fury over his humiliating incarceration and unwilling to give any of the gang members the satisfaction of knowing just how hopeless he felt his situation to be.

Chapter Five

Shortly after dawn on the third of June, twenty-one-year-old Jenny Moore left her room at the Antlers Hotel in Rock Springs, Wyoming, carrying her luggage. She was making her way down the narrow hallway toward the stairs when a door opened a few feet ahead of her and two men carrying handbags stepped out. Both of them smiled and greeted her cheerfully.

Jenny greeted them in return. They had boarded the stage with her in Denver five days before, and she had enjoyed their company. Both well-dressed and good-looking men in their midthirties, Lloyd Nordell and James Bateman were escorting thirty thousand dollars in cash from the Colorado Savings Bank in Denver to a new bank that was opening in Jackson. Wells Fargo had contracted to transport the money and had assigned Nordell and Bateman to guard it for the length of the trip. Along with some important papers, the money was being transported in a regular suitcase in the boot of the stagecoach, while the strongbox under the driver's seat held three hundred dollars and some official-looking papers as a ploy to throw off any robbers who might stop the stage along the way.

The taller of the two reached out his hand. "May I carry your bag, Miss Moore?" James Bateman asked.

"Thank you," she replied.

As Bateman took the suitcase from the young woman, Nordell commented, "You look fresh as a daisy, even after all that time on our dusty stagecoach, Miss Moore. You must have slept well last night."

"As soundly as Rip Van Winkle," responded Jenny, "only not quite as long. Although I confess that after having to sleep on the stage the previous four nights, I could easily have stayed in that wonderful bed for another whole day."

Both men chuckled appreciatively as they escorted her the rest of the way down the hall.

Descending the stairway, Jenny's comely form attracted the attention of several men who were standing about in the lobby. Strikingly beautiful, she stood five feet five and had a shapely, well-proportioned figure. She was neatly clad in a medium-gray full-length dress that had white lace adorning the high neck and a matching cuff of lace at the wrist. A small hat was perched on top of her honey-blond hair, which tumbled in a long fall behind her head, accentuating her femininity.

As they reached the lobby, James Bateman said, "I assume, Miss Moore, that you'll be eating breakfast in the hotel dining room."

"Yes." She nodded.

"May we have the pleasure of your company?"

"You may," Jenny said with a smile.

The threesome moved toward a table in the mostly empty dining room, noticing their stagecoach crew, driver Eli Crowell and shotgunner Wyatt Andrews, breakfasting as well.

"Good morning, Mr. Crowell, Mr. Andrews," Jenny said, smiling politely at the crewmen as she reached their table.

The middle-aged Crowell and his young shotgunner were sitting with two other men, and all four men rose quickly to their feet.

"Good morning, Miss Moore," Crowell responded, running his fingers through his brown hair in an attempt to smooth it.

Wyatt Andrews cleared his throat and said, "Miss Jenny Moore, I would like you to meet the two additional passengers who will be joining us for the ride to Jackson.

This gentleman is Mr. Cletus Holmes, and this is Dr. Dale Barnett."

Holmes, a withered little man in his late seventies, greeted Jenny with a toothless smile. The very handsome doctor, who was quite blond himself, was of medium height and build and looked to be about thirty. He held out his hand, which Jenny shook.

"I'm delighted to meet you, gentlemen. Are you traveling to Jackson on business?" Jenny asked.

"I'm afraid my business days are behind me," Holmes responded. "Actually, I'm returning home to Jackson after visiting some relatives here in Rock Springs."

"I suppose you could say I'm going to Jackson on business," Dale Barnett said. "I've left the Kansas City hospital where I was working to take over the practice of Jackson's only physician, who's retiring."

"Well, it's very nice to make your acquaintances. Now if you'll excuse us, we'd better eat our breakfasts as well. We wouldn't want to hold up the departure of the stage."

The sun was over the eastern horizon, and the crew had the stage ready to go. As the passengers prepared to board, James Bateman said to the driver, "I know I've cautioned you before, but I like to be on the safe side. There's no chance that the suitcase with the money can fall out of the boot, I assume."

"No, sir," Crowell said and grinned. "She's packed in there tighter than a steer in a stockyard pen."

Bateman nodded as the other passengers neared the stagecoach.

Wyatt Andrews approached Jenny Moore and offered his hand. The young shotgunner had been hypnotized by her beauty from the moment she had entered the Wells Fargo office in Denver. With a big smile, he said, "May I help you aboard, Miss Moore?"

"Why, thank you, Mr. Andrews," she said, returning the smile and accepting his help. She settled in her seat, and as the men boarded, Jenny wished for the presence of the pleasant matron who had ridden the stage from Denver to Rock Springs, where she was met by her husband. Jenny suddenly felt very outnumbered.

As the stage rolled out of Rock Springs heading north-west, Jenny watched the scenery pass by. It was wildly beautiful prairie at this point, dotted with sandy bluffs and rock formations amid patches of scrub oak and a sea of sagebrush. Her attention was drawn back inside the coach when Dale Barnett said, "Miss Moore, forgive me if I'm being impertinent, but you know why Mr. Holmes and I are going to Jackson, while we have yet to learn why you're traveling there."

Light danced in Jenny's deep-blue eyes as she smiled at the young doctor sitting directly across from her and replied, "I am going to Jackson to marry the most wonder-ful man in the world, Doctor."

"Well," cackled Cletus Holmes, "I guess you boys can relax then, can't you?"

There was a round of laughter, and then the doctor said, "Who is the lucky man, Miss Moore?"

"His name is Lobo Lincoln," replied the rosy-cheeked beauty.

Raising his eyebrows, he said, "Lobo? That's the Span-ish word for wolf, isn't it? Is your fiancé part Spanish or Mexican? I presume it'd be only part, since Lincoln is an Anglo-American name."

Shaking her head, Jenny smiled and replied, "Actu-ally, Doctor, you're wrong on both counts. Lincoln is not his real name—I mean, it is not the name he started out with in life. It came from the fort at which his father was stationed. You see, Lobo is half Indian—his mother was an Arapaho. She—" Jenny stopped and looked at the two guards. "Oh, but you two have already heard this. I don't want to bore you with this story again."

"Whether they're bored or not," Dale said with a grin, "I want to hear all about this Lobo Lincoln."

"As do I, pretty lady!" exclaimed Cletus Holmes.

"We don't mind hearing it again," said Lloyd Nordell. "It's a fascinating story."

"Indeed it is," James Bateman agreed.

Jenny's face tinted. "Really, gentlemen, I don't want to be the center of attention, here. I—"

"You already *are* that, ma'am," said the outspoken Holmes, "so you may just as well go ahead and tell the story."

Jenny blushed shyly and took a deep breath. "All right," she sighed. "But stop me if you've heard enough." Shifting slightly in her seat, she began, "Well, I think I'll describe Lobo first. That makes it easier to comprehend the rest of his incredible story," she declared, pride in her voice. "He's six-feet-six-inches in his bare feet. By the time he puts on his boots and dons his hat, he looks as though he's as tall as an oak—and as sturdy as one, too, since he weighs about two hundred and fifty pounds."

Dale Barnett gave a low whistle.

Jenny smiled at the doctor's reaction and then told them of Lobo's various careers. "He was a pathfinder across the western wilderness for wagon trains and hunting expeditions—that's how we met—and he's fought hostile Indians as an army scout. He was also a buffalo hunter, and for the past few years, he's been a special agent for the government, tracking down criminals." She smiled again and looked shyly down at her hands folded in her lap. "But all that adventure will be coming to an end. Lobo just took a job as ranch foreman near Jackson because he wants to settle down to a normal life once we get married."

Cletus Holmes cackled, "I'd say being married to a gorgeous female like you will be adventure enough, my dear!"

Jenny's face colored vividly while the younger men laughed and agreed with the oldster.

Dale Barnett came to her rescue and changed the subject. "You said that Lobo's half Arapaho and that he took his name from a fort? Did I understand that correctly?"

Laughing sympathetically with the doctor at his confusion, Jenny explained, "You see, Lobo's mother lived with her people along the banks of the Cannonball River near Fort Abraham Lincoln, and his father was a sergeant in the Army, stationed at the fort. Lobo doesn't know how his parents met, or anything about their courtship, but they fell in love and were married. His father took his wife away from her tribal village to a home just outside of the town of Bismarck, near the fort. After Lobo's parents died, when he was two years old, the whites didn't want anything to do with the child because he was a half-breed."

"Why, that's shameful!" the doctor declared, looking outraged.

"Yes, it is," Jenny agreed, nodding her head. "The fort officials took him to the Arapaho village where his mother had lived and left him with the Indians. The whites didn't even tell the Arapahoes the child's name, so his mother's people named him Little Sparrow."

"Little Sparrow, huh?" interrupted Cletus Holmes. "From what you've just told us about Lobo's size, whoever named him wasn't thinking too far in advance."

Everyone laughed, and then Jenny continued.

"When Little Sparrow was old enough to understand, the Indians told him about his past, but no one could remember what his father's name had been. They did remember that his mother had been very beautiful, and that his father had been a giant of a man.

"By the time Little Sparrow was sixteen," proceeded Jenny, "his people had moved west to Colorado, settling on the plains not far from the Rocky Mountains. One day he was riding alone on the plains, carrying a single-shot rifle, when he came upon a pack of wolves trying to kill a young antelope." She paused a moment, running her eyes over the faces of the men, and then she said, "Lobo told me that for as long as he can remember, it has always angered him to see sides unbalanced in a fight or a struggle. When he saw all those wolves attacking that lone antelope, he was furious. He slid from his horse and fired a shot into the air, hurrying to go to the antelope's aid."

"But many animals hunt in packs. It's nature's way of providing food for them," the doctor interjected.

"Yes, I know," Jenny said, "and Lobo understands that and respects the ways of nature. But he was very young at the time, and he reacted to what he thought then was a terrible injustice.

"At the sound of the shot, the other wolves fled," she continued. "But the largest male wolf, which was the leader of the pack, was not scared off, and the animal ran toward Little Sparrow, fangs bared, and attacked. There wasn't time to reload the rifle before the wolf hit him full-force, but of course by that time Little Sparrow was not so little. He already weighed two hundred pounds and was very strong. He battled the maddened beast with his bare hands and managed to choke the wolf to death, but not before the animal's sharp fangs had slashed his face, hands, and arms." Jenny paused, and a loving look appeared on her face. "He still bears the scars from that battle on his right temple and cheekbone."

"My goodness," Dale Barnett declared, "that's quite a tale. What happened then?"

"As Lobo tells it, he was bleeding badly and passed out after killing the wolf. Some Mexican buffalo hunters found him lying next to the dead wolf, and they revived him and carried him back to the Arapaho village. While the Arapaho medicine man worked on Little Sparrow's wounds, the Mexicans commended his strength and courage, and dubbed him Lobo, explaining that in their language the word meant wolf. The name stuck.

"A few months later, when Lobo decided to leave the shelter of the Arapaho village and make his way in the white man's world, he knew he would need a last name. He wanted to identify with his parents, but not knowing what their last name had been, he took his name from Fort Abraham Lincoln, where his father had served as a soldier. From that day on, he's been Lobo Lincoln."

The stage pulled into a relay station where the six lathered horses would be exchanged for six fresh ones. As it pulled to a stop, Cletus Holmes smiled broadly and said, "Well, little lady, your tale has made this journey back far more enjoyable and go a lot faster than the trip out. Thank you for such fine entertainment."

"I certainly hope you haven't finished your story," Barnett said and grinned. "I want to hear how you and this amazing Lobo Lincoln met."

"All right, I promise to tell that part of the story as soon as we get back on the road again."

The passengers alighted from the coach and stretched their legs, and then they and the crew were served a crude meal in the cramped interior of the relay station. After climbing back into the coach and starting the next segment of the journey, Jenny noticed that she was seeing many more trees as they moved northward. She also noticed that dark clouds now covered the sun, and the wind was picking up. Fearing they were in for a storm, she hoped it would not cause a delay in the trip.

Over the loud clacking of the wheels, James Bateman reminded Jenny, "You were going to tell Dr. Barnett and Mr. Holmes how you and Lobo met, Miss Moore."

"Yes, please do. As I recall, you said something about a wagon train?"

"Yes, that's right." She paused and then said, "I guess I should begin at the beginning. I am originally from Gary, Indiana. My father decided to move us to the frontier and begin a new life, so two years ago last March, we left Gary and headed west, joining a small wagon train at Lawrence, Kansas. By early June, we were on the Colorado plains a few miles east of the Rockies when a war party of two dozen Cheyenne renegades attacked us. There were only eleven men in our wagon train, so we were easily overpowered."

The young blonde choked up briefly, but then regained her composure and proceeded. "The Cheyennes . . . first killed the men and boys . . . including my father and younger brother. Fortunately, when the attack had first begun, my mother had hidden me behind some large boxes in our wagon, because the Cheyennes then massacred the women and girls, too. It . . . it was horrible. I could hear their screams and cries as they were killed with tomahawks and knives. I was terrified. When the screaming was over, I knew everyone, including my mother, was dead. I lay there, hoping the Indians would not look in the wagon or set it on fire. When I heard the war party riding away, I thought it a miracle I had survived and hadn't been discovered. I—"

The stagecoach suddenly stopped and Eli Crowell called down from the box, " 'Scuse me, folks, but you'd better drop the curtains. It's starting to rain pretty hard." Getting into his slicker, he started up the coach again.

Wind-driven rain began to fall, and James Bateman and Dale Barnett unrolled the leather curtains over the windows. Then they looked expectantly at Jenny for her to continue with her story.

"I crawled out of my hiding place in the wagon, thinking the Cheyennes were gone, not knowing that three warriors had been left behind and were looting the wagons. One of them spotted me and shouted to the others." She suddenly shuddered at the memory. "Standing next to the wagon was a pinto that I guessed belonged to one of the dead Indians. In desperation I jumped on it and raced away, but the Indians gave pursuit on their ponies.

"The next thing I knew, they caught me and were dragging me from the pinto. I was certain my life was over. But suddenly, as if out of nowhere, a huge dark-skinned man thundered in and fought off the attackers, killing them." She smiled brightly and said, "Of course, the huge man was Lobo Lincoln. He was returning to Denver from New Mexico on a government assignment."

Tears came into her eyes as she continued, "Lobo placed the bodies of my family in our wagon and drove it to the nearest town, where we had them buried in the cemetery. Then he took me to Denver, where he found me a room in a boardinghouse and got me a job in the restaurant of the Brown Palace Hotel."

The wind started howling so loudly that Jenny could barely be heard. As the rain violently lashed the coach, the passengers rode in silence as Eli Crowell kept the team at a steady pace despite the storm.

Cletus Holmes saw the worried look on Jenny's face and shouted above the noise, "Don't worry, this storm will soon be over. Rainstorms like this are normal for this part of the country, and they never last very long."

The old man was soon proven correct. Within twenty minutes the wind ceased, the sun came out, and the storm was over. The leather curtains were rolled up, and the air smelled fresh and clean.

Another relay station came into view. The passengers and crew refreshed themselves while the team was being changed, and soon the stage was moving again.

Dale Barnett, eager to hear the rest of Jenny's story, said to her, "I assume you and Lobo got to know each other after you settled in Denver."

"Yes," she said and smiled warmly. "Every time he was in town between government assignments, he came to see me. Soon we both knew we had fallen in love. Our love just grew stronger and deeper as time passed." A dreamy look came into Jenny's blue eyes. She laid her head back against the seat and sighed, "Lobo proposed to me when he was last in Denver, three months ago. He said he would give up the adventurer's life and settle down if I would become Mrs. Lobo Lincoln."

"How long did it take you to decide to say yes?" asked the doctor.

Jenny snapped her fingers. "About that long! Lobo told me he had been offered a job as foreman of the Flying M Ranch, which is a bit north of Jackson, when he had been in Jackson Hole last September. He rode up here a couple of weeks ago to see if the job was still open, and it was. He wired me that he had been hired, and that I should take this stage to Jackson. We're going to be married tomorrow."

Dr. Dale Barnett eased back in his seat and smiled. "That's a beautiful story, Miss Moore. Congratulations. I hope you and Mr. Lincoln will be very, very happy."

"Thank you," she responded warmly.

"Do you plan to have a family?"

"Oh, yes. Lobo loves children. He wants a houseful, and so do I."

"Well, good," exclaimed the doctor. "Child delivery is one of my specialties. I also treat croup, whooping cough, measles, chicken pox, mumps, and all other things that are common to little boys and girls. If your sons are as rough and tough as their father, they'll probably have a few broken bones along life's way. But don't worry—I can take care of those, too."

Jenny giggled. "I see you have a great deal to recommend you, Dr. Barnett."

"Even if I didn't," the young doctor said with a smile, "I feel reasonably certain of your business."

"Oh? And why is that?"

"Because according to Dr. Tomlinson, whom I am replacing, I will be the only medical doctor within seventy-five miles of Jackson."

Throwing her head back and laughing delightedly, the lovely blonde said, "Well, in that case, Dr. Barnett, I can assure you that you will definitely be the Lincoln family's physician."

When the laughter had died down, the men settled into conversation about the growth of the West and its future in the life of the United States, while Jenny watched the breathtaking terrain outside.

The stagecoach had already crossed the Snake River several times, and it was now weaving its way among some beautiful mountains. Jenny had noted that the scenery was increasingly dramatic as they moved northward, though they were still many miles from Jackson Hole and the Tetons. Lobo had said that Jackson Hole—with the Tetons, the forest, and the Snake River—was the most beautiful place in the whole world to him, and he told Jenny that she would feel the same. She was beginning to see why he felt that way.

A short time later Jenny was awakened from a nap when Eli Crowell shouted down to his passengers, "We're gonna be crossing over the Snake on a brand-new bridge in about ten minutes. As soon as we get to the other side, you'll know we're exactly five miles from Jackson."

The winding river shone like liquid gold in the light of the late afternoon sun, and Jenny felt her heart quicken pace when she realized she would soon be in the strong arms of the man she loved. Looking past the hills just ahead of them, she could see the green expanse of a broad, sweeping valley. This was undoubtedly the south-

ern tip of Jackson Hole, and she was thrilled that this was
going to be her new home.

Up in the box, Eli Crowell and Wyatt Andrews were
discussing how full the Snake River was running for so
early in the spring when the new bridge suddenly came
into view. "There she is," exclaimed Crowell. "That there
beautiful structure sure makes it a lot easier to get to the
other side of the river than it used to be."

But fifty yards from the bridge, four masked men
rushed out from the trees. Two of them stood in the road
aiming rifle muzzles at the driver and shotgunner; the
other two, wielding revolvers, approached the stage from
both sides as Crowell braked rapidly to a halt. The driver
looked over to his left at the bulky frame and ugly face of
the man who bellowed, "Get those hands in the air! Fast!"

Crowell could sense that Andrews was bristling. From
the corner of his mouth, he said, "Don't even think of
resistin', son. The big guy is Gavin Brubaugh, and he's
about as cold-blooded as they come. He shoots first and
thinks later. Get your hands in the air."

Andrews set his double-barreled shotgun at his feet
with the muzzles pointing skyward and lifted his hands.

Inside the coach James Bateman peered out the window and said in a low voice, "Robbers!" He and the other
guard whipped out revolvers from their shoulder holsters.

But at that instant one of the outlaws appeared at the
window and barked, "Throw them guns out here, you two!
We got your driver and shotgunner in our gunsights, and
if we get one lick of trouble out of any of you in there,
they're gonna die!"

Prepared for just such an occurrence as this, Bateman
and Nordell both carried derringers under their belts, as
well. They did as they were ordered and tossed their
revolvers out the window, waiting for an opportunity to
use their concealed weapons.

"Okay," one of the outlaws said gruffly. "Everybody
out. Come slow and come with empty hands, or you're
dead. Line up alongside the stage. Now!"

Lloyd Nordell whispered, "Doc, you stay close to

Miss Moore and Mr. Holmes. Protect them the best you can if shooting starts."

Dale Barnett nodded.

Jenny whimpered. She had not known such fright since the day the Cheyennes had attacked her wagon train.

As the passengers began to file out, Brubaugh circled around the back of the stage, looking it over. Then he came around to the side, where two of his men now stood, and the ugly giant first beheld Jenny Moore. He caught his breath. For several seconds he stared at her as if stunned.

Finally pulling his gaze from her, Brubaugh said to a cohort, "Get their money and jewelry. Uh . . . that is, except the woman's. Leave her alone."

The outlaw's jaw went slack. "What are you talkin' about? The jewelry she's wearin' has gotta be worth somethin', and she's probably got money in her purse, too."

Fire leaped into Brubaugh's eyes. "Shut up and do like I tell you!" With that, he looked up at Eli Crowell and said, "Okay, driver, I want you to hand me down the strongbox. Fast! Come up with a gun, and you've kissed your wife for the last time!"

While one of the outlaws relieved the men of wallets, watches, and stickpins, Brubaugh took the strongbox from Crowell's hands and set it on the ground. Without bothering to ask for a key to the padlock, he shot it off.

Brubaugh dug into the metal box, throwing the papers into the breeze. When all he came up with was three hundred dollars, he swore. Stuffing the bills in the pockets of his overalls, he glared angrily at Eli Crowell and snapped, "Where's the thirty thousand?"

"What thirty thousand?" Crowell asked with feigned innocence.

Shaking his gun at the driver, Brubaugh blared, "Don't play dumb with me, fella. You know what thirty thousand. The money for the new bank that's openin' up in Jackson next week."

"Mister, somebody's steered you wrong," Crowell said levelly. "We ain't got no bank money."

The outlaw holding the rifle on the driver from in front of the stagecoach walked toward his leader and said, "Gavin, maybe he's tellin' the truth."

Nordell and Bateman eyed each other, their hands still in the air. Was Gavin Brubaugh going to buy it?

Brubaugh looked over at the outlaw who had spoken. "Foss, get back there and keep your gun on those two in the box!" he shouted. "R. W., you come here and help me. We're going through every piece of luggage and every piece of cargo on this stage."

Crowell felt his spine go cold as Brubaugh glowered at him and rasped, "If I find out you lied to me, driver, I'll kill you!"

The young shotgunner, convinced that Brubaugh meant what he said, blurted, "He's only doing his duty, mister! Please don't hurt him. The thirty thousand is in a dark brown suitcase in the boot."

Brubaugh swung his gun on the driver and fired without warning. Eli Crowell gave a slight grunt as the bullet ripped into his chest, and then he peeled off the seat and hit the ground with a dull thump.

When James Bateman saw that the outlaw directly in front of him had turned his attention to the driver's falling body, he knew he would get no better chance to use the derringer hidden in his belt. Reaching for the gun, he aimed it at the outlaw. Lloyd Nordell was a few seconds behind him, going for his own derringer.

Bateman's gun roared, and the outlaw went down with a bullet in his chest. Brubaugh and the one he had called R. W. both shot James Bateman at the same time.

Dale Barnett quickly pulled Jenny Moore and Cletus Holmes to the ground. Lying on the ground just inches away from where Bateman fell, Jenny saw the terrible wound and began screaming.

Another of Brubaugh's men had shouldered his rifle and swung it at Nordell just as the guard was aiming his derringer at Brubaugh. The man pressed the rifle's trigger, and the slug punched a ragged, scarlet hole in Nordell's head. He went down like a rotted tree in a high wind.

Anger raging through him, Wyatt Andrews repeat-

edly eyed the shotgun at his knee, but he could not reach
for it: The fourth outlaw was aiming a cocked rifle straight
at him.

As the smoke cleared, Brubaugh saw that both guards
and the driver were dead. So was one of his men. It was
evident that the shotgunner and the other passengers
were not going to offer any resistance.

Dale Barnett stood up and helped Jenny to her feet.
The young woman was having a hard time catching her
breath. Cletus Holmes was also struggling to stand, and
Dale bent down to give him a hand.

Brubaugh commanded Fred Foss to search the boot
and find the suitcase. Eager to have the robbers gone,
Wyatt Andrews said, "I'll get it for you."

Moments later, the young shotgunner handed the
suitcase to the outlaw, and Brubaugh opened it, taking a
quick look inside and grinning greedily. Snapping the
suitcase shut, he handed it to Fred Foss and said, "You
carry this, 'cause I won't have room for it. I'll be ridin'
double."

Accepting the suitcase, Foss eyed him quizzically.

Then the outlaw leader turned to Jenny and, showing
his filthy teeth in a repulsive smile, said, "You're comin'
with me, honey."

The blond woman's face went a ghostly white. Shaking her head, she said defiantly, "I . . . I am not! I'm not
going anywhere with you!"

Brubaugh made a move for her, but he was blocked
by Dale Barnett, who had thrown caution aside and stepped
between them. Shoulders squared, the doctor said stiffly,
"You got what you wanted. Leave her alone!"

"The money ain't all I want, now!" raged Brubaugh,
attempting to shove Dale aside.

But the doctor did not budge. His body was rigid
with determination, even in the face of Brubaugh's revolver, which was now cocked and leveled between his
eyes.

Wyatt Andrews stepped in crying, "Wait!"

Brubaugh turned and looked at him.

"Doc, don't buck him!" the shotgunner said. "Eli told

me about him. He'd as soon kill you as he'd step on a cockroach."

"You got that right," said Brubaugh. Grinning at Dale, he breathed hotly, "Now back off, mister, or you get a bullet in your head."

The doctor realized he was hopelessly outnumbered, and he could possibly get Jenny killed if he tried anything else. Standing beside the shotgunner and the trembling Cletus Holmes, Dale watched helplessly as the gang rode away, taking with them the bank money, the body of their dead friend, and a terrified Jenny Moore.

Chapter Six

Earlier that afternoon, Lobo Lincoln had left the Flying M Ranch in time to ride to Jackson and meet the stage that was carrying his bride-to-be. Since the stage was to arrive at six o'clock, Lobo looked forward to sitting down to a celebratory dinner with Jenny Moore in the nicest restaurant in town.

Guiding his sorrel across the valley, the big man was once again struck by the majesty of the towering Tetons. There were a few white clouds gliding near the snow-covered pinnacles, adding a touch of splendor to their awesome beauty. Since he had started working at the ranch and got to see the mountains daily, he had noticed that the sheer rock walls and jagged peaks of the Tetons seemed to be constantly changing, and they were so big that they made their own weather. Lobo could see storms raging on the main peaks while down here in the valley a couple of miles away, the sun shone brightly.

The big half-breed studied the massive mountains in solemn reverence as the sun cast shadows across the craggy faces of granite and schist. Soon they would melt into the solid purple shades thrown over the Tetons when the sun dipped behind the mountains for the night.

When he heard one of the ranch hands say that he was hoping someday to climb Grand Teton, the highest peak of what was known as the Cathedral Group, Lobo had thought the man was kidding, but the cowboy swore that back in 1872, two climbers had actually made it to the top. Shaking his head as he rode near the peaks, Lobo marveled at the thought of trying to scale hundreds of feet of sheer escarpment.

He put the sorrel into a steady trot again, heading straight south, with the winding banks of the Snake River to his left. Soon he would hold his beautiful Jenny in his arms . . . and the next day she would be his wife.

Lobo grinned broadly as he looked around. The grass seemed greener, and Jackson Hole looked better than it ever had; the flowers smelled prettier; the sky looked bluer . . . in fact, the whole world was better. Lobo Lincoln had found the love of his life, and she was about to become bone of his bone and flesh of his flesh.

It was twenty minutes before six when Lobo dismounted in front of the Wells Fargo office. Ducking his head and entering, he found agent Bob McGee behind the counter at his desk. McGee looked up and said, "Howdy, Mr. Lincoln. I'll bet you're excited."

"I sure am, Mr. McGee. When the stage arrives and you get a look at Jenny, you'll understand why."

"Oh, by the way," McGee said, shoving his chair back and standing up. "I have a telegram for you." Pulling open a desk drawer, he said, "Frank Willoughby brought it over here this morning. I knew you'd be coming by this evening, so I held on to it."

"Thanks," Lobo said, taking the yellow envelope from the agent's hand.

Tearing open the flap, Lobo saw immediately that the telegram was from William Kettering of the U.S. Office of Territorial Affairs in Denver. The few lines informed him that a detailed letter would be arriving on the June third stage, and that Lobo should respond to the letter as soon as possible.

Lobo smiled to himself, figuring Kettering's letter would be an eloquent appeal, listing reasons why he should not resign his position as special agent for the government. He found it amusing to think that a letter asking him to stay on as a government agent would be delivered on the very stage that was also delivering the reason for his quitting.

Folding the telegram and stuffing it into his shirt pocket, he said, "Well, Mr. McGee, since I'm a bit early, I'll take a walk over to the general store and visit with John Holland for a few minutes. I assume you're expecting the stage to be on time."

"Sure am," answered McGee, "so don't stray too far."

"With Jenny coming in, a herd of bison couldn't keep me away from here. Don't worry, I'll have one eye on the office all the while I'm at Mr. Holland's store. See you shortly."

Nearly an hour had passed when McGee looked up to see Lobo Lincoln duck his head and enter the office again. There was concern on the big man's face as he asked, "Why do you suppose the stage is running so late?"

"Well, it's not all that unusual for it to be delayed," answered McGee calmly. "Lots of times it'll run an hour or so behind. Rainy weather sometimes causes it. A horse can throw a shoe. A wheel can come off. There are several things that can—"

McGee's words were interrupted by the sound of galloping hooves, spinning wheels, and the rattle of harness.

"Aha!" he exclaimed with a grin. "There it is now!" He followed Lobo outside onto the boardwalk. The big man had a broad smile on his face as the stage rolled toward the office, but Bob McGee knew something was wrong when he saw that Wyatt Andrews was driving the team and Eli Crowell was not beside the shotgunner in the box.

Then Lobo noticed the lone man up top, and a look of concern replaced his smile when he saw the expression on the young shotgunner's face.

The stage squealed to a dusty halt with Andrews already shouting, "We got held up! They killed Eli and the two Wells Fargo guards!"

Lobo's heart went to his throat, and he hurried toward the door of the stage.

As Andrews was climbing down, the door popped open and Dr. Dale Barnett alighted, followed by Cletus

Holmes. Lobo looked past them and saw three bodies inside the coach, but there was no sign of Jenny. Vaguely he heard the shotgunner saying something to Bob McGee behind him as he put his hand on the arm of the blond man and said, "Miss Moore, Jenny Moore. Was she on this stage?"

Dale knew who the man was from his dark color and size. "You must be Lobo Lincoln. Yes, your fiancée was on the stage." He swallowed hard. "I wish I didn't have such terrible news, but the men who robbed us took her with them."

The doctor's words hit Lobo like a battering ram, and cold fury rose up inside him. "Was anyone else taken? Were there any other women?"

"No, sir, Miss Moore was the only one. I don't think her life is in danger, although I suppose you could look at that as being even worse. You see, the leader of the gang seemed captivated with her. I think he'll want her alive."

Lobo's massive frame shook with rage, and his blood began to boil. He grabbed Dale Barnett's arm and demanded, "Mister, you've got to give me a description of the robbers and take me to the spot where they stopped the stage. How far back was it?"

Wyatt Andrews stepped up to Lobo and said, "It was only five miles back, Mr. Lincoln. And I know who the robbers are. It's the Brubaugh gang."

Lobo Lincoln knew the reputation of Ma Brubaugh's blood-hungry bunch. "Was the old woman with them?"

"No, sir. But Gavin Brubaugh was there. He's the one who took Miss Moore. I know it was him because Eli—he was our driver—said so just before Brubaugh shot him."

Lobo gripped Andrews's shoulder. "You've got to take me to the spot right now!" he almost shouted. "I've got to get on their trail immediately! I can't leave Jenny in their hands one minute longer!"

Wincing under the powerful grip, Andrews replied, "It'll be dark by the time we get there, Mr. Lincoln, and the gang went eastward into the forest. I know the moon's almost full, but there's too much cloud cover tonight to be able to read the tracks clearly. I'll be glad to take you out there first thing in the morning."

Lobo suddenly realized he was hurting the young shotgunner and released him quickly. Blinking, he said, "I'm sorry. Sure. You're right, fella. I . . . I just wasn't thinking clearly. But the thought of Jenny out there with those heartless beasts . . ."

The blond man spoke up. "Mr. Lincoln, I am Dr. Dale Barnett, and I've come to Jackson to take over Dr. Noah Tomlinson's practice. May I say that your Jenny is one of the finest young women I have ever met, and if you would permit me, I would like to go along with you in the morning. I'd like to help you find her."

"Thank you, Doctor," said Lobo, trying to give him a smile. "I appreciate your offer, but I need to handle this myself."

"I understand." Dale nodded. "But if you should change your mind and want company, you can find me at Dr. Tomlinson's place."

Lobo thanked him again, then turned to Andrews and said, "I want to leave at first light, young fella."

"My name's Wyatt Andrews, Mr. Lincoln," said the shotgunner, "and that's fine with me. I'll meet you right here in front of the office at dawn."

"See you then." Lobo started to walk away.

"Oh, wait just a minute, Mr. Lincoln," called Andrews. "There's some mail for you in the box. I'll get it."

Andrews hopped up to the box, lifted a canvas bag from the floor, and returned. Fishing in the bag for a few seconds, he brought out a large tan-colored envelope and gave it to the big man. Lobo ripped open the envelope and looked over the three wanted posters that were included with William Kettering's letter. The posters bore photographs of Ma, Gavin, and Hecky Brubaugh. There was a five hundred dollar reward for Hecky, and one thousand each on Gavin and Ma. On all three posters, the reward was offered dead or alive.

The accompanying letter informed Lobo of Governor

Roger Whitson's assassination by the Brubaugh gang, and that U.S. Marshal Patrick Day and his deputy had left Rock Springs in pursuit of the gang the day after the assassination. They had not been heard from since. Lobo shook his head. *Almost two weeks have gone by*, he said to himself. *Both men are probably dead by now.*

Reading further, Lobo found Kettering begging him to set aside his new job long enough to track down the Brubaugh gang and bring them to justice, enlisting whatever help he could muster.

Lobo shook his head at the horrible irony. *Of all the people in the world Kettering wants me to go after*, he thought, *it's the scum who have Jenny!*

Kettering added that the Brubaughs were wanted dead or alive, and it would not upset the authorities at all if they were brought in dead. Lobo's Arapaho upbringing normally kept him from using profanity, but he breathed an oath and said under his breath, "If they've hurt my Jenny, it will definitely be dead!"

With rage flowing through him like molten lava, Lobo found the telegrapher, Frank Willoughby, walked him to the telegraph office, and had him send a wire to William Kettering in Denver. When Kettering opened his office in the morning, he would know that Lobo had accepted the assignment.

From the telegraph office the big half-breed went to John Holland's apartment above the general store. After apologizing for disturbing him, he told Holland what had happened and explained that he needed to buy ammunition for his Colt .45 and his Winchester .44. He also needed some food and trail supplies.

Holland took him downstairs and into the store, filling a cloth sack with everything Lobo needed. When the big man was ready to leave, Holland asked, "Where you going to sleep tonight?"

"I figure I'll just take my horse to the livery stable and sleep in the hay loft," replied Lobo.

"Nonsense, I won't hear of it. I insist you stay here," offered Holland. "We've got an extra bed, although your feet may hang over the end a bit."

"Thanks very much. I'll take it," Lobo said, forcing a slight smile onto his lips. "After I deposit my horse at the livery and find someone in town who'll take a message out to Mr. Muller at the Flying M for me, I'll be back." Jamming a hand into a pocket of his faded denims, he pulled out a wad of bills and asked, "How much do I owe you for the supplies?"

"Nothing," Holland assured him. "Let these few items be my part in helping to find your Jenny."

"You're a good friend, Mr. Holland. I really appreciate all your help."

"I'm glad to do it for you, and I think it's time you call me John," the shopkeeper said, putting his arm on Lobo's shoulder. "When you come back, we'll have a meal fixed for you. I'll also ask my wife to fix you a good breakfast in the morning. You'll need strength for what lies ahead of you."

Lobo took his horse to the livery, then went to the Elkhorn Saloon, where he found a couple of cowboys from a ranch that bordered the Flying M. He gave them the details of his situation, and they agreed to stop by the Muller ranch on their way home and give Mr. Muller a message from him. His tasks completed, Lobo headed back to John Holland's apartment.

The fury inside him was growing stronger. He told himself that if he had to rip out every tree in the Teton Forest, he would find Jenny . . . and if Gavin Brubaugh had laid one of his dirty hands on her, he would wish he had never been born.

As darkness fell over the Teton Forest, Dora Phillips and Lois Crane were in the kitchen of the Brubaugh gang's hideout, preparing the evening meal. Hecky Brubaugh sat on a stool at the end of the table, his eyes fixed on Lois as she moved about the room. His presence made her uneasy, and his constant surveillance was playing havoc with her nerves.

Dora was aware of how Lois was feeling, and with her

own nerves on edge, the redhead stopped stirring the stew and turned to the hulking man. "Hecky, you really like Lois, don't you?"

A slow grin worked its way across Hecky's blunt face, and his dull eyes sharpened. Nodding, he said, "I sure do, Dora. I like Lois a whole lot. She's my girl."

"Then you wouldn't want to upset her, would you?"

Lois was watching from the corner of her eye, wondering what Dora was up to.

"Uh-uh," replied Hecky. "I wouldn't want to upset her."

"Well, you *are* upsetting her by sitting there watching every move she makes. Why don't you go out on the porch where everyone else is? Maybe they're talking about something interesting."

Hecky, looking at Lois and then back at Dora, said sharply, "If Lois wants me to go out on the porch, let her tell me that."

The pretty brunette looked at Hecky and said, "Yes, Dora's right. You are making me nervous, and I would like for you to go out on the porch."

"Okay," he said, sliding off the stool. "But if you need me, Lois, you call me."

"I will," she assured him.

Once Hecky was gone and the two women were left alone, Dora hurried to Lois's side and said, "Thank God he left. Lois, what are we going to do? We've got to find some way to get away from these awful people."

"I agree. I was hoping Marshal Day would be able to find a way, but being shackled to the post out there day and night, he hasn't got a chance." She shook her head and added, "The poor man. It's inhuman, the way they're treating him. Even when they take him to the privy, he's handcuffed and outnumbered, so making a break is impossible."

Dora stirred the stew vigorously with the wooden spoon as she said sadly, "I don't think Ma Brubaugh is going to let him live much longer. I heard her say something about it to Hecky this morning."

"I was afraid it might come to that," sighed Lois. "I just feel so helpless." Pausing, she said, "How long till that stew is finished?"

"Probably ten minutes."

"Everything else is ready. I'm going to take some of this salve I found in the cupboard and put it on the marshal's wrists. Those cuffs have chafed the skin till it's raw."

Taking the tin of salve, she went outside onto the porch where Ma and her men were sitting and smoking by the light of two lanterns.

Ma peered out into the darkness of the vast forest and said angrily, "Where in the devil's Gavin? He should've been back here by now. I hope to tarnation that fool son of mine hasn't gotten himself into trouble. If he has, I'm gonna tan his hide!"

"Don't worry, Ma," Carl Blade spoke up. "He and the boys will be here soon. Are you forgettin' it's thirty miles or better to where they were plannin' to pull the robbery? And a good part of their return trip is bein' made in the dark. They probably won't get here for another couple of hours yet."

"They might even be later," suggested Herman Tarver. "Them stagecoaches ain't trains, you know. They often run real late. Gavin and the boys might have had to wait awhile. Who knows?"

Ma Brubaugh, who was short on patience, went on grumbling about Gavin's tardiness, but she had calmed down somewhat. Suddenly she noticed Lois walking meekly across the porch and barked at her, "Hey! What're you doin' with that salve?"

Without pausing, Lois walked over to Patrick Day and explained what she was going to do. "It might relieve his suffering."

Ma pulled a fresh cigarette out of her bib pocket and flared a match with her thumbnail, saying no more. She just took a deep pull on the cigarette and watched.

The lawman seemed to read the pity on Lois's face as she knelt down beside him. A faint smile appeared on his drawn and haggard face, which now had a scraggly growth of beard that made him look even worse. "I appreciate your kindness," Day whispered hoarsely.

Hecky Brubaugh's eyes were riveted on Lois as she opened the tin of salve and gently applied it to the marshal's wrists. He did not like her giving such attention to another man. Resentment began to build in him when she did not leave the marshal immediately after she had finished administering the ointment, but instead, attempting to give Day some measure of comfort, talked quietly to him. Hecky let it go for another three or four minutes, but still Lois stayed beside the marshal.

When Dora appeared at the door and called them to supper, Lois stood up and said to Day, "I'll bring your food to you right away."

That was too much for Hecky Brubaugh; normally one of the men brought the marshal his meals. Becoming furious, Hecky stood up and screamed at Lois, "You get away from him! You've been there long enough. Somebody else can bring him his supper. You hear me?"

When the young woman did not comply, Hecky exploded. He stomped over to her, a fierce glow replacing the usual dullness in his eyes. Then his huge right hand lashed out and struck a powerful backhanded blow.

Lois flew off the porch and hit the ground. Dazed, she sat up, holding her reeling head as Hecky bellowed at her from the edge of the porch, "You're *my* girl, Lois! Do you hear me? *My* girl! I don't want you ever payin' attention to any other man! If you ever do it again, I'll beat you to a bloody pulp!"

Patrick Day's anger blinded his caution. "Leave her alone, you filthy animal!" he yelled.

Showing his teeth like fangs, Hecky swore and kicked the marshal in his mouth.

Day's head snapped back as blood spurted from his lips. While the others cheered him on, Hecky drew back his foot, swore again, and with the roar of a wild beast, kicked Day in the chest. Breath gusted from the marshal's mouth, spraying more blood.

"That's it, son!" Ma shouted. "Let him have it!"

Lois had risen to her feet. Staggering, she screamed, "No, Hecky! No more! Please stop!"

But the slow-witted oaf was half out of his mind. Turning toward Lois, his mouth a hard, unrelenting slit, he railed, "You're *my* girl!" Then he stepped off the porch and backhanded her once more. Lois reeled backward and again fell to the ground.

Still in a mindless rage, Hecky returned to the marshal, whose head was lolling loosely on his neck, and chopped his jaw with a hard right, then a left. Day went unconscious, sagging against the handcuffs that held him to the post, and Hecky kicked him in the head.

Ma Brubaugh stepped up to her son, who was breathing hard. She patted his shoulder, and said with elation, "Atta boy, Hecky. I guess you showed that tin star a thing or two! That woman ain't very nice to you. Maybe we ought to get rid of her."

Hecky's wrath was cooling now that he had vented it sufficiently on the lawman. He turned and looked at Lois, who lay half-stunned near the edge of the ring of light provided by the burning lanterns on the porch. "No, Ma," he said slowly. "Lois is my girl. She'll be good now."

Dora Phillips ran from the doorway, where she had stood witnessing the whole thing. Rushing past the outlaws, she knelt, put her arm around Lois, and helped her to her feet. Even in the dim glow of the lanterns, Dora could see the welts on Lois's face and her swollen lower lip. "Come, my dear," she said tenderly. "Let's get you into the house."

Ma watched the two women as they moved into the cabin. Then to the men she said, "Let's go eat."

Sitting Lois on a chair near the door, Dora bathed her face with a wet cloth while the outlaws sat down and began to eat. She ignored as best she could Hecky's constant glances in Lois's direction.

"I'm proud of you, son," Ma said through a mouthful of food. "You handled that lawman just fine."

Herman Tarver spoke up and said, "Ma, I don't see

any reason to keep that stinkin' marshal alive any longer. Seems to me if any more lawmen were gonna show up, they'd have been here by now."

Lois and Dora listened fearfully. There was no way they could prevent Patrick Day from being cold-bloodedly murdered.

"Our greatest danger ain't from the law, anyway, Ma," Carl Blade suddenly blurted out, without thinking. "It's from Iron Jaw."

Tarver choked on the mouthful of stew he had just swallowed. His head jerked up and he looked at Ma Brubaugh, whose mouth had just clamped shut like a trap. A red flush washed over the big woman's face as she glared at Blade.

Fear stamped itself visibly on Blade's face as he realized what he had just said.

Slowly Ma Brubaugh lifted herself out of her chair and stood over Blade menacingly. Narrowing her eyes, she demanded, "What did you mean by that, Carl? Why are we in danger from that renegade Indian?"

Blade looked nervously at Tarver, whose face was white with dread. There was no sense lying; it was too late for that. Stammering out the story, he told Ma about her son's killing Tall Tree and wounding Red Feather.

When he had finished, the old woman stared at Tarver and shouted, "Herm, is he tellin' it like it happened?"

"Yeah, Ma," confessed Tarver, unable to look her in the eye. "That's the way it was."

The flush on Ma's face was deepening in color. "Why wasn't I told about this?" she screamed, throwing down her fork.

"Gavin threatened us," gasped Blade. "He made us swear not to tell you."

"Yeah, Ma," put in Tarver, "we didn't want Gavin mad at us."

The ponderous woman exploded into a rage, swearing vehemently and shattering the chair she had been sitting on with a heavy kick. Her eyes bulging, she ran her arm across the table, sweeping everything onto the floor. Then she stormed around the cabin, calling her son every foul name she could think of, and started smashing up the furniture.

"I'll kill every last one of you cowards," she threatened. "You're gonna regret not tellin' me the truth!"

Dora and Lois ran and huddled in a corner. Hecky, Blade, and Tarver tried to calm Ma down, but then backed up against the nearest wall, deciding instead to stay out of her way.

Her rage ending after a few minutes, Ma looked over the mess in the cabin, gasping for breath. Then she turned to the gang members and said, "We gotta pack up and get outta here. It's a wonder Iron Jaw ain't sneaked in here and massacred us already. We're pullin' outta this place at first light, Gavin or no Gavin. I'll deal with him later, if that bloody redskin don't kill him." Then she snorted angrily and added, "It'll serve him right if he does."

"But what about the thirty thousand dollars Gavin and the boys took off that stage today?" asked Blade. "You just gonna leave without gettin' it?"

"We can't spend it if our scalps are hangin' on Shoshone belts!" snapped the big woman. "Now you three—load guns, ammunition, and supplies in the wagon so's we can be ready to go at dawn." Turning her attention to the women, she commanded, "What are you two waitin' for? Start cleanin' up this mess. And I want breakfast cooked tomorrow mornin' before we leave."

"What about the lawman out there?" asked Tarver.

"You let me worry about him," growled the big woman. "Just set about doin' what I told you."

As the three men filed out the door, Ma limped to a crude cabinet that was secured with a padlock. Pulling a key from her pocket, she opened the lock and took out a rifle.

Lois and Dora eyed each other frantically as she disappeared through the door. Seconds later the report of the rifle racketed through the forest.

"Dora!" gasped Lois. "She killed him! She killed the marshal! They're all merciless beasts!"

"I knew it was coming," said Dora, putting a shaky hand to her mouth. "She'll do the same to us before this is over. We've got to get away!"

With trembling hands, Lois started picking up the smashed crockery and scattered utensils that littered the room.

Dora cast a quick glance toward the door, making sure no one was watching. Then, terrified and desperate and unnoticed by Lois, she grabbed the butcher knife sitting on the counter and hid it in the deep pocket of her skirt. She herself would kill Ma if necessary.

Chapter Seven

Lois and Dora heard a sudden shout from outside. "Hey, Ma, look over there. Gavin's back."

"Well, it's about time!" Ma Brubaugh fumed. "At least Gavin's done something right—or he'd better have. If he don't have that thirty thousand, I'm tying him up to one of these posts and leavin' him here for Iron Jaw to find. Then his corpse can join that lawman's."

She stood up, folding her meaty arms across her massive chest, waiting for the men to ride across the clearing.

"What the—" she began, startled to see a young blond woman riding in front of Brubaugh on his horse. Then she spotted the lifeless form of one of her men, Art Wilson, draped across his horse. She said menacingly, "I guess Gavin ain't done somethin' right after all. Looks like he messed up real bad."

The group rode up to the cabin, and as Brubaugh dismounted, she snapped, "What happened to Art?"

"We had some resistance when we held up the stage, Ma," replied her son. "Had to kill three men. Art caught a bullet durin' the fracas; but look what Fred's got there in his hand. That suitcase has thirty thousand dollars in it!"

"Gimme it," she grunted, stepping up to Foss. Taking it from his hand, she moved back over to Brubaugh and said icily, "And what do you think you're doin' by bringin' this blond hussy here? Ain't you got no sense at all?"

"She ain't no hussy, Ma!" he snapped angrily. "She's my woman!"

"What do you mean she's your woman?" Ma retorted. "You don't have no woman unless I say so! Where'd you get her?"

"Took her off the stage. Ain't she the most beautiful female you ever laid your eyes on?"

Ma looked up at the terrified Jenny and bawled at Brubaugh, "I don't care if she's the Queen of Sheba! I don't want her around here!"

"But Ma—"

"Don't give me no sass, boy! You're gonna have to get rid of her, so take her out into the woods and kill her. Then you march yourself right back here, because I got me a bone to pick with you."

Panic clutched at Jenny's heart. She could feel the pulse throbbing in her neck and temples, and she felt as though she was going to faint.

Although the moonlight did not reach into the deep overhang of the porch, she could see by the lantern light the bloodied corpse of Patrick Day, and a cold chill ran up her spine. She knew that this man who had kidnapped her was brutal, but she had held out a sliver of hope that perhaps the mother he had spoken of would have some compassion. Now she knew better—and she felt doomed.

Gavin Brubaugh's anger struggled to erupt like a volcano. He wiped his hand across his mouth and then clenched it into a fist, swinging it through the air. Cursing vehemently, he barked at his mother, "I ain't gonna kill her, Ma! If Hecky can have a woman, I can have one, too!"

Leaning from the saddle, Jenny said with trembling voice, "Please, Mrs. Brubaugh, I didn't ask to be brought here. Please, just let me go. I'll *walk* out of here; I don't care. Just let me go!"

Brubaugh's face tightened. "You ain't walkin' out of here, Jenny, and Ma ain't makin' me kill you, neither. You're gonna be my woman."

"I said she ain't!" Ma blared.

Brubaugh looked down at his mother and said through

clenched teeth, "Ma, I ain't givin' in on this. I deserve the same as Hecky gets—"

"I'll tell you what you deserve!" she roared. "You deserve to be drawn and quartered!"

"What the devil are you talkin' about, Ma? I pulled off this job just fine. It ain't my fault that Art got taken down. And the assassination went off just as we planned. We—"

"That's not the way I heard it," Ma growled menacingly. Looking over at Jenny, she ordered, "You! Get off that horse!"

Brubaugh turned and walked toward his horse, saying, "I'll help her down and take her in the house."

Ma drew in a deep breath and then let it out through her nose. "You do that, boy," she said with disgust. "Then you and me are gonna settle things."

"Settle what, Ma?"

"Just get her in the house and come on back out here."

Brubaugh felt Jenny's body trembling as he roughly took her down from his horse. Planting her feet on the ground, he took her by the hand and pulled her into the cabin. He led her over to Lois and Dora, who stood watching from the kitchen.

Letting go of her hand, he said, "You stay in here with these two. They know better than to try to run away. Ask them what'll happen if you do."

The huge man lumbered back out onto the porch, half closing the door behind him as he went out.

Lois and Dora gathered around Jenny, each briefly taking one of her hands, and introduced themselves. Speaking softly, the frightened blonde said, "I knew you two were here. Those horrible men talked about you while we were riding. My name is Jenny Moore."

"We heard Gavin say he took you off the stage," said Dora.

"Yes." Jenny sighed deeply and nodded. "Just a few miles before Jackson, where I was supposed to be married tomorrow."

"Oh, how awful for you!" Lois exclaimed.

"What about you?" Jenny replied sympathetically. "How many days have you been held captive by these brutes?"

Dora shook her head. "I've almost lost count by now. Every minute seems to be an eternity."

"Surely we'll be found soon," Jenny said hopefully. "If we can just hold out here a little longer without being harmed or—"

"I'm afraid that finding us is going to become harder," Lois interjected. "Even Gavin doesn't know it yet, but we're leaving here at dawn. All of us."

"Why? Where are we going?"

"While they were bringing us here from Steamboat Springs, Gavin killed a Shoshone Indian and wounded another," said Lois. "The old woman just found out a little while ago from a couple of the men who were in that group. She's fearful that their chief will show up and massacre all of us for what Gavin did. She hasn't said where we're going—I'm not sure that she knows yet."

Jenny frowned. "I thought all the Shoshone were on reservations."

"These are renegades," replied Dora, "and they refuse to stay on the reservation. From the way they talk, this Chief Iron Jaw must be a very vengeful man."

"Oh, dear Lord, we've just got to get out of here. We've got to get away from these horrible people!" moaned Jenny. "What happened to that poor man handcuffed out on the porch?"

"The old witch murdered him just a little while ago," Dora said grimly. "He was a U.S. marshal."

Jenny bit her lower lip and shook her head, trying desperately to hold back her tears.

Just then they heard Ma Brubaugh's voice rising, yelling at someone. The words were indistinct, but they could tell she was furious.

"Getting away from the Brubaughs will be no easy task," declared Lois, "but I'm willing to give it another try if we can—"

Lois's words were cut short by the terrible shouting coming from outside, and the three women moved closer to the front door to hear what was being said and see what was going on.

Ma was standing with her hands on her broad hips, staring at her elder son, her mouth set in a stern line.

Carl Blade stood stiffly next to Herman Tarver, while Brubaugh glared at him, barely keeping his rage in check. "So you went and squealed to Ma, huh?"

Trying to act as nonchalant as possible, Blade inched his way over to Art Wilson's horse, making as if he were inspecting Wilson's bullet hole. "Well, it wasn't quite that way, Gavin," he began. "It—"

"Never mind who said what," Ma blurted. "The only thing wrong with what he told me was that he should have told me the minute you got back from Colorado. Who's runnin' this gang, Gavin, you or me?"

Brubaugh stared at the bulky figure standing in front of him. Despite his size, her brutal ways had filled him with fear all his life. He was feeling that same intimidation scratching at his insides at that moment, but he was not going to let her know it. Keeping his deep voice level, he replied, "You always ran the gang, Ma."

"I didn't ask you who *ran* the gang," she blared. "I asked you who's runnin' it *now*!"

Brubaugh hated his mother at times. Being browbeaten was bad enough, but to have it done in front of the men was almost more than he could bear. His mouth went dry as he said, "You are, Ma. You're running the gang."

"Well, you sure got a peculiar way of showin' it."

"But Ma—"

"Don't 'but Ma' me, Gavin Brubaugh! You've done some dumb things in your life, but nothin' like pullin' a harebrained stunt like shootin' a Shoshone buck in the head and wingin' another one when it wasn't necessary. Because of your stupidity, we all gotta pack up and get outta here." As she spoke the last words, she unleashed a solid, open-handed slap across her son's face that echoed like a gunshot across the clearing and through the darkness of the surrounding forest.

The huge man's head snapped sideways from the

blow, and although his eyes filled with fire, he stood like a statue.

Ma hissed at him through her teeth, "Didn't you stop to think that killing that Shoshone would bring that bloody Iron Jaw right to our front door with massacre on his mind? I don't know what's takin' him so long to get here. It's a wonder we ain't already been killed and scalped, thanks to you. I oughtta kill you myself for what you did!" Again she slapped him violently.

Brubaugh took the blow without budging an inch, although his face felt as if it were on fire. With a hatred welling up within him that was almost tangible, he said in a quiet, deadly voice, "The reason Iron Jaw hasn't been here is 'cause I covered our trail real careful. He ain't gonna show up."

"Don't give me that guff, you bunglin' idiot. You're too stupid to outsmart an Indian. I tell you he'll be here, and we gotta be gone when he comes."

"Okay, so maybe we gotta pull out," her son said gruffly. "Maybe it's time we was movin' on anyway. Just quit hittin' me and callin' me names."

Her face flushing deep red, Ma's eyes blazed as she growled, "I'll say and do whatever I please. Seems you need to be reminded who's boss of this outfit." Shouting over her shoulder, she said to her other son, "Hecky, go get my whippin' strap!"

Hecky's beefy features blanched. "Please, Ma," he gasped. "Don't whip Gavin. Please!"

"Shut up and get the strap, Hecky. If I have to get it myself, I'll whip you, too!"

Fear was in his dull eyes as Hecky Brubaugh wheeled and shuffled onto the porch, opened the door, and stepped into the house.

Inside, the three women stood huddled together, terrified. They watched Hecky go over to a peg and pull down a wide leather strap about four feet long with wicked-looking six-inch knotted strips on one end. Following behind Hecky, they stood near the open doorway as he went outside and shuffled over to his mother, who was standing opposite her elder son, the two facing each other like angry grizzly bears.

"I'm warnin' you, Ma," Brubaugh said, "I ain't takin' no more beatin's."

Timidly, Hecky handed his mother the strap. With her jaw set, she wrapped the solid end of the strap around her right hand, leaving about three feet of leather dangling. "Shootin' them Indians was bad enough, Gavin," she said, her voice grating roughly, "but keepin' it from me . . . You've got a big lesson to learn." Clenching her teeth, she raised her arm to strike the first blow.

But Gavin, suddenly erupting in fury, shot out his left hand and seized her wrist.

Ma Brubaugh was shocked. Her son had never before dared to resist her. She grunted and tried to free her wrist, but it was held tight. She breathed heavily, snarling, "You worthless skunk. I wish it was *you* the vigilantes had hung instead of your brother!"

While holding her wrist with one hand, Brubaugh pulled the strap from her grasp with the other. His eyes were wild as he said ferociously, "I'm gonna show you what it feels like, Ma!"

Releasing her abruptly, Brubaugh lashed her across the face with the strap. The big woman staggered backward from the impact, shaking her head and blinking in disbelief as red welts surfaced on her leathery face. She emitted a cry that sounded like that of a wounded cougar and came at her son with both fists clenched, but he struck her with the whip again, and blood ran down her face and neck and spewed from her mouth.

Hecky Brubaugh stood wringing his hands, not knowing what to do. Ma had laid the strap on him more than once when she felt he had had it coming, so he knew what it felt like, and he did not blame his brother for trying to stop her from using it on him. But he could not bear watching his mother getting beaten.

The three women looked on from the doorway, numb with shock at the terrible spectacle. Just beyond them, out on the porch, the other gang members kept looking at each other, not daring to make a move; Gavin Brubaugh was completely uncontrollable.

Lois suddenly realized that everyone was mesmerized by the scene outside. She turned to Dora and Jenny, breaking their spellbound awe. "This may be our chance to get away," she whispered. "When we're sure nobody is looking this way, we can slip out and run into the forest. The darkness can hide us."

Jenny and Dora agreed, and the three of them braced themselves and waited for the perfect moment to make their escape. Moffitt, Foss, and Tarver had their attention riveted on Ma and Gavin, but the women were within their line of sight. Any movement on their parts might get the outlaws' attention; they dared not run yet.

Then Gavin Brubaugh let out a murderous groan. Throwing aside the leather strap, he raised his clasped fists over his head and brought them down violently on his mother's shoulder, knocking her to her knees. He began punching her again and again, beating her into bloody submission. The giant's ponderous strength was more than even his sturdy mother could endure, and she fell to the ground.

"Gavin, stop!" Hecky shouted, rushing over to his brother. "Don't hit her no more, Gavin! She's bleedin' read bad!" The slow-minded young man grabbed his brother's arm.

Brubaugh shook off Hecky's grip. "Shut up!" he shouted. "Don't tell me you liked it when she beat *you* up!"

"No, but you've done enough, Gavin. You gotta stop now!"

Brubaugh looked down at his mother. She lay helpless, waving her arms weakly. "I haven't done enough yet, Hecky," he snarled. "Not quite enough." Insane with anger, he dropped to his knees, and closing his huge hands around his mother's throat, he began to squeeze the life out of the old woman.

Her eyes wide in disbelief and anger, Ma kicked and tried to pull her son's hands from her neck. But his grip was too strong; eventually her struggles subsided, and she lay motionless, strangled to death.

When Brubaugh finally got up and stood over her body, he hissed, "I just couldn't take it no more, Ma. I just couldn't take it!"

Hecky knelt down and touched his mother's shoulder. Looking into her open eyes, he said, "You can get up now, Ma. Gavin ain't gonna hurt you no more." When she did not move, Hecky shook her limp arm and repeated louder, "You can get up now, Ma!"

Foss, Moffitt, Blade, and Tarver looked at one another and shook their heads. They stepped off the porch, going to Hecky's side, their backs to the cabin.

Lois realized their chance had come. She looked at Dora and Jenny and whispered, "Let's go!"

Grabbing their long skirts to keep them from swishing, the three women scuttled out of the door and moved stealthily toward the dark forest.

Fred Foss laid a hand on Hecky's shoulder and said, "Come on, Hecky. Your ma's not gonna get up. She's dead."

Not quite comprehending, Hecky lifted his head and turned to look up at Foss, and in doing so, he caught sight of the women just as they left the ring of light surrounding the cabin. Suddenly forgetting his mother, he jumped to his feet and shouted, "Hey, Lois, where are you goin'? Don't run away! Come back here! You're my girl!"

Brubaugh and his four men whirled around as Hecky took off after Lois. Shooting a quick glance toward the house, Brubaugh shouted, "Grab a couple of lanterns, fellas! We can't let them women get away!"

Within seconds, the remaining gang members were dashing toward the forest, and Ma Brubaugh lay alone in the dim circle of light from the remaining lantern, a lifeless smudge on the unfeeling ground.

There was very little moonlight entering the dense forest, and the women were finding it difficult to pick their way through the blackness. They knew they had immediately been spotted making their escape, and above the noise their feet and their skirts were making, they could hear the loud voices of all the men in pursuit. Looking back periodically, they could see the lanterns, glowing and bobbing among the trees like giant fireflies.

Hecky Brubaugh was well ahead of the others. He was staying close on the heels of the women by listening for their movements as, breathing hard from their exertion and their fear, Lois, Jenny, and Dora pushed deeper into the forest.

Hecky called to Lois repeatedly, begging her to stop. By the loudness of his voice, the women could tell he was gaining on them.

"Hurry!" puffed Lois. "He's getting closer!"

Not having the same stamina as the other women, Dora started slowing down. Jenny realized she had dropped back and called over her shoulder, "Dora, are you all right? Come on!"

"I'm right behind you!" Dora gasped.

Hecky heard the women calling to each other, but the noise of his own feet drowned out the words. Then he made out a vague form directly in front of him, and the huge man shouted, "Lois!" and lunged for the woman, his strong fingers closing on her shoulders.

Dora screamed and struggled to shake loose of his grip. Frantically, she whipped out the butcher knife from her skirt pocket and drove it into Hecky Brubaugh's side with all her might.

Hecky howled wildly as the blade went in almost up to the haft, just missing his bottom rib.

Dora felt him buckle. She let go of the handle and turned to run, but her feet tangled in her long skirt, and she fell to the ground.

Lois and Jenny stopped when they heard Dora scream and then Hecky howl. Jenny said breathlessly, "Hecky must have caught her. We've got to help her."

"Yes," agreed Lois, and they began groping their way back through the trees.

Grimacing with pain, Hecky stayed on his feet, hovering over Dora like some huge bird. While she scrambled to rise, he yanked the knife from his side and came down on top of her with one powerful lunge. Growling like a maddened beast, he started stabbing her, and Dora screamed in agony as Hecky plunged the knife into her again and again.

Jenny and Lois had almost reached them just as the other outlaws rushed up with their lanterns. Standing just beyond the lantern light, they could make out Hecky down on his knees stabbing Dora. Then she stopped screaming and lay still, and Hecky dropped the knife, clutching his bleeding side. A moment later he fell over on top of her.

Jenny gasped, clamping a hand over her mouth. "She's dead," she whispered into Lois's ear.

Lois released a tiny whimper and, sucking for breath, said, "Come on. We've got to get away."

But the outlaws were too close. Just as the women wheeled to run, the men spotted them and gave chase. Gavin Brubaugh seized Jenny, and R. W. Moffitt grabbed Lois, dragging the two women over to where Herman Tarver knelt over Hecky.

Looking up at Gavin Brubaugh, Tarver said, "Dora must have stolen a knife. She stabbed him but good, and he's bleedin' pretty fierce."

"Let's get him back to the cabin," Brubaugh said solemnly. Gesturing toward Dora, he said, "Leave that one for the animals."

"You can't just leave her here," Jenny protested. "She needs to be buried."

"You're lucky we don't bury you two right now," Brubaugh growled. "Come on!"

The two women were dragged roughly through the forest, fighting with their free hands to keep the branches from whipping their faces. Shoved through the cabin door, they were locked in the bedroom that Lois and Dora had been sharing.

Tarver and Blade carried Hecky back to the cabin and laid him on the dirty, ripped sofa in the main room of the cabin. While Gavin Brubaugh worked at stopping the flow of blood from his brother's wound, Fred Foss said, "Gavin, I think your ma knew what she was talking about. Indians *are* expert trackers, and it's a wonder Iron Jaw hasn't found us by now. We've gotta get out of here as quick as possible."

"You're right," he agreed. "I guess I wasn't thinkin' too clearly, was I? Ain't no sense takin' chances." He rubbed his bearded jaw. "Tell you what. You and R. W. ride into Jackson right now and get that old doc. It'll be hard for Hecky to travel, but we'll have the doc sew him up here, and then we'll take the doc with us. He can take care of Hecky as we travel."

"Sounds like a good plan to me, Gavin," Foss agreed, and knowing there was no time to spare, the two men ran to the corral and saddled their horses, galloping out of the yard and heading for Jackson.

Hecky Brubaugh regained consciousness while his brother was wrapping his side with cloth, and watching the two brothers from the doorway, Carl Blade stood contemplating his own fate. He was glad Brubaugh had not sent Herman Tarver for the doctor, since Blade's only hope was that Tarver would be able to convince Gavin Brubaugh not to harm him.

Hecky ran his dry tongue over his lips and mumbled, "I want some water."

"Bring him some water, Herm," Brubaugh said over his shoulder.

Tarver hurried to the kitchen and lifted off the dipper hanging on the side of the water bucket. Filling the dipper, he brought it over to Brubaugh.

"You give it to him, Herm. A few sips at a time. I got other business to take care of."

Tarver looked sharply at Brubaugh and then knelt down beside Hecky.

When Brubaugh turned around and stared at Carl Blade, his eyes like cold steel, Blade's body stiffened and his heart froze in his breast. His lips were bloodless as he stammered, "G-Gavin, what was I supposed to d-do? Ma was—"

"You just went and blabbed off about me killin' that stinkin' redskin, didn't you?"

"N-no, Gavin. It wasn't like that. It . . . just slipped out. Ask Herm. Tell him, Herm!"

Whipping out his revolver and snapping back the hammer, Brubaugh rasped, "How about if I let my thumb just slip off this hammer, Carl?"

Herman Tarver looked over at Blade, who stood there pleading with him to come to his defense, but Tarver was not willing to endanger himself over Blade. Brubaugh was in a killing mood. Without a word, Tarver turned his head and focused his attention back on Hecky.

"Herm!" shouted Blade. "You said you'd reason with Gavin!"

"Nothin' to reason about, Carl," said Brubaugh.

"L-listen, Gavin, y-you can have my share of the money from the stagecoach! And . . . and from the assassination, t-too!"

"Don't make no difference, Blade," Brubaugh smirked. "With you dead, I get it anyway, don't I?" Grinning evilly, he said, "Say good-bye, Carl." Then he dropped the hammer.

The gun roared, and the impact of the slug slammed Carl Blade against the doorframe. Hanging there for a moment like a marionette on a string, he then slid slowly down the frame, leaving a crimson trail all along its edge. He landed in a sitting position and then fell sideways, his head cracking heavily against the floor.

Brubaugh eyed the dead man impassively and then turned to Herman Tarver. "We gotta be ready to pull out as soon as the doc's fixed Hecky up," he said as if nothing had just happened.

"Ma had us loadin' the wagon before you got here," said Tarver, equally implacable.

"We ain't takin' the wagon. Too easy for Iron Jaw to follow. We'll put packs on a couple of horses, and we'll need two other horses as well. Jenny's comin' with us, and we'll need one for the doc, if he comes out here in his buggy."

From his place on the sofa, Hecky said weakly, "Lois has to come, too. Don't forget a horse for Lois, Gavin."

Brubaugh looked over at his younger brother and

sighed. "Okay, Hecky, your woman can go. But she better not try anything stupid." He looked over at the closed door to the bedroom where the two women were still imprisoned.

"Where we goin'?" Tarver asked.

"North," replied Gavin, breaking his revolver open and punching out the spent shell. As he slipped a fresh cartridge from his gun belt and inserted it, he said, "Up into Montana. We'll stay in the forest as much as possible for protection, then cut east and pick up the South Fork River. Most of the winter snowmelt will be gone by now, so it'll be shallow enough to ride the stream for a while to keep Iron Jaw from trackin' us. Once we get into the mountains there, there ain't no way that bloody redskin is gonna find us. Then we'll cross over into Montana, and with the money Ma had hoarded up here, plus the ten thousand from the killin' and the thirty thousand out there in that suitcase, we'll find some real out-of-the-way town and be able to live like kings for a long, long time." He glanced back at the bedroom door again and said, "Yeah, I think that'll be mighty appropriate, since the minute I saw my woman, I said to myself that she looked just like a princess."

Jenny Moore and Lois Crane sat on the edge of the bed in their room, their arms around each other, trying to comfort and be comforted. At the sound of the gunshot, they ran to the door and peered through a knothole. Jenny had been horrified at the sight of Carl Blade's bloodied body, and she had sat back down again, feeling weak-kneed. "That man is completely heartless," she said, lamenting their terrible situation. "Poor Dora. Such a horrible way to die, and we can't even give her a decent burial."

Shaking her head, Lois said wistfully, "I don't know if there's any chance now of getting away from these animals. They're going to watch us closer than ever. I guess the best we can hope for is that they won't kill us." Suddenly thinking about being touched by Hecky's repulsive hands, she shuddered and added, "Then again, maybe dying *isn't* the worst thing that can happen."

Jenny pushed the same sickening thought from her mind. "Do you think we'll still be leaving here?" she asked.

"Your guess is as good as mine," replied the pretty brunette. "Gavin didn't seem worried before about Iron Jaw showing up here, but maybe the old woman's fear will make him think differently."

Jenny patted Lois's hand. "Either way, I've got to keep hoping that this horrible nightmare will end before too long."

Blinking quizzically, Lois asked, "What do you mean? If the authorities had sent additional lawmen out after the marshal and his deputy when they didn't return or report in, then they must have lost the trail, or they would have found us by now."

"Do you remember that I said I was supposed to be getting married tomorrow?"

"Yes."

"Well, my intended's name is Lobo Lincoln. Up until recently, he made his living tracking down outlaws for the government, and there isn't a man in the West who can out-track him. I can guarantee you that when Lobo learned I had been abducted, he started after the gang—and he won't quit until he rescues me. Even if we pull out of here in the morning, Lobo will find me."

Hope appeared in Lois Crane's eyes. "You sound quite certain your Lobo Lincoln can save us."

"Not a doubt in my mind," Jenny said with assurance.

"Then all we have to do is stay alive and . . . un-harmed until he finds us."

Jenny suddenly felt ill. "That's all," she said weakly.

Chapter Eight

Dr. Dale Barnett was asleep in the spare bedroom of Dr. Noah Tomlinson's house when he was awakened by a loud knock at the front door. He sat up in the bed, trying to decide whether he had imagined the sudden, startling noise. Then the knock was repeated, and he heard the elderly physician stirring in the next room.

The young doctor quickly climbed out of the bed and fumbled in the dark for the matches that he had left on the nearby dresser. Finding them, he struck one and lit the kerosene lamp, reading the time on the pendulum clock on the opposite wall. It was twenty past two.

Pulling on his pants and tucking in his nightshirt, he picked up the lamp and opened his bedroom door at the same time as Dr. Tomlinson opened his.

The heavy knock was repeated a third time.

"You go on back to bed, son," said the wrinkled old man, his face lit by the lamp that he was carrying. "No sense in both of us getting up."

Dale shook his head in disagreement and said, "I may just as well get used to this. It'll be my job shortly, after all."

Tomlinson walked to the front door without comment while Dale stepped back to the end of the hallway to leave his lamp on a small table. The elderly physician flipped the lock and pulled the door open, lifting the lamp he carried to get a better look at the two men who stood on the porch.

"Good morning, gentlemen. What can I do for you?"

"We're from the Box D Ranch, about twenty miles southwest of here, Doc," Fred Foss lied, looking from Tomlinson to the person standing behind him. Dale Barnett's back was to him and R. W. Moffitt, and all they could see was his size and shape. "One of our ranch hands had an accident and got cut badly. We're afraid he's in real bad shape, and we need you to come with us and see what you can do for him. He'll probably die if you don't."

"Oh, my, we can't have that, can we?" Tomlinson said. "Just let me get dressed."

"No, Dr. Tomlinson, that's too long a journey for you to make," Dale Barnett said, looking at the elderly doctor as he stepped up beside him. "I'll be glad to go, gentlemen. I'm—"

Dale and Foss recognized each other simultaneously. Foss drew his gun quickly and thumbed back the hammer. "You! You mean you're a doctor?"

Tomlinson turned to his replacement and asked, "Do you know these men?"

"Yeah," breathed Dale, looking from Foss to Moffitt, then at Tomlinson. "I told you about the stage being held up."

"Yes."

"These two were part of the gang that did it."

Foss snapped impatiently, "I asked if you were a doctor!"

"Yes, I am. I've come here to take over Dr. Tomlinson's practice. He's retiring."

Foss grinned wickedly and said, "Okay, Doc, then you can be the one to go with us. I'm sure you can handle the trip much better than this oldster here."

Moffitt moved in close and said, "We'll have to kill the old man, Fred. Otherwise he'll scream his head off when we ride outta here. Next thing we know, there'll be a posse on our tails."

Tomlinson stiffened, and Dale said quickly, "There's no need for that! Why don't you just tie him up? It'll be hours before anyone finds him. I assume you lied about where you're from, so he can't tell anyone in which direction we've gone."

Foss and Moffitt exchanged glances. Then Foss said, "Okay, we'll tie him up. You hurry up and get dressed," he ordered the younger doctor. "R. W., go with him and make sure he don't try anything funny."

Ten minutes later, the outlaws rode out of Jackson with their prisoner after stealing a horse and tack from the livery at the edge of town for the doctor to ride. As they picked their way through the dark forest Dale Barnett said, "I'm concerned about Jenny Moore. Is she all right?"

"She's fine," Fred Foss replied curtly. "Don't worry yourself. She ain't your concern, anyhow. She's Gavin's woman, and he'll take good care of her."

Dale was quiet for a moment and then said, "Were you lying about someone being badly cut, or is that really why you're taking me with you?"

"We got a man stabbed, Doc. I was only lyin' when I said it was accidental. Your Jenny Moore and two other women tried to run away from us. One of 'em had grabbed a butcher knife from the kitchen, and when Gavin's brother, Hecky, tried to catch her, she put the knife in him. He ain't doin' so good."

Dale swallowed hard. "What happened to the woman?" he asked, almost afraid to learn the answer.

"Little wench got what she deserved," R. W. Moffitt declared. "Before he collapsed, Hecky pulled the knife out of himself and stabbed her to death with it."

"But no one harmed the other two women?"

"Nope," responded Moffitt. "Leastways, not up to the time when we left. Gavin locked 'em up in one of the bedrooms."

"Guess we might as well tell you now, Doc," Foss said. "You'll be goin' on a little trip with us."

"What do you mean?"

Foss told him about the incident with the Indians. "There's the danger that Iron Jaw will show up with blood in his eye. So we're pullin' out first thing in the mornin'."

"That could be perilous for the wounded man," said the young physician. "If he's hurt as badly as you say, traveling could kill him."

"That's where you come in, Doc," said Moffitt. "It'll be up to you to keep Hecky alive while we travel."

Dr. Dale Barnett felt a cold, hard ball settle in his stomach. He had heard and read much about the desperadoes in the West. What he had seen at the stagecoach holdup had been a firsthand lesson about their cruelty and disregard for others—and he was afraid to find out what the next lesson might be.

The sun was long over the eastern horizon when the three men rode across the clearing to the hideout and saw the two packhorses tethered to a pine tree with their backs fully loaded. Ma Brubaugh's crumpled form still lay on the ground where she had died, while Carl Blade's body had been dragged across the porch and lay close to the dead U.S. marshal. Dale Barnett eyed the corpses uneasily as he dismounted, black bag in hand.

"Don't pay them no mind," said Foss. "Hecky's the only one you need to look at, and he's in the cabin."

At that instant, Gavin Brubaugh's hulking frame appeared in the doorway. As Foss pushed the doctor toward the cabin, Brubaugh's eyes narrowed. "What'd you bring *him* for?" he growled at Foss.

"Recognize him?"

"Yeah. He was on the stage. Where's the doc?"

"This *is* the doc," Foss said with a grin. "He's takin' over the old guy's practice. I figured you'd rather have a young healthy guy travelin' with us than an old geezer who's about to bite the dust."

Brubaugh's frown disappeared. "Oh. Well, yeah, that's good thinkin', Fred." As Dale stepped up on the porch, Brubaugh asked, "What's your name?"

"Dale Barnett. I want to know if Miss Moore is all right."

" 'Course she's all right!" Brubaugh thundered. "She's my woman, and I don't let no harm come to my woman." He grabbed Dale by the arm and pulled him into the cabin. "Did Fred tell you about Hecky?"

"Yes."

He gestured toward his bleeding brother and ordered, "He's hurtin' bad, Doc, so get to work on him."

Herman Tarver was seated next to Hecky. As Dale came farther into the room, Tarver stood up and said, "He's passed out again, Doc. He's been in and out ever since it happened."

Sitting down on a stool next to the sofa, Dale began tending his patient. Foss and Moffitt were hovering over the couch, and the young physician looked up at them and said, "I'd appreciate it if you would take yourselves off somewhere, gentlemen. You're not making my job any easier."

"Go check on the horses," Brubaugh told them. "Make sure the cinches are good and tight. And R. W., get the women out here and have 'em start breakfast."

Standing near the sofa and watching the doctor peel away the blood-soaked cloth that he had earlier applied to Hecky's wound, the huge outlaw flinched as Dale cleaned the oozing puncture with alcohol and began stitching it up. He was glad Hecky was unconscious. While the physician worked, Brubaugh said, "I guess the boys already told you we're pullin' up stakes and movin' out of here, Doc."

Concentrating on his work, Dale merely nodded. He finally tied a knot in the catgut and exclaimed, "There. I'm finished."

"Good. I guess you were also told that you're going along."

The young physician looked up at the outlaw and cocked his head. "How much does your brother's life mean to you, Mr. Brubaugh?"

The huge man's back stiffened and his mouth turned down. "I suppose you think because I killed my ma that my brother don't mean nothin' to me."

"I don't know anything about your killing your mother," said the doctor without looking up. "But—"

"You mean Fred and R. W. didn't tell you about me stranglin' Ma?"

"No—and to tell you the truth, I don't think I want to know. The reason I asked about Hecky is because if you make him travel, he'll die. He shouldn't be moved for at least a week, and even then it would be questionable."

"That can't be helped, Doc," grumbled Brubaugh. "We're pullin' out of here as soon as you're finished tendin' him." Pivoting, the outlaw stomped out of the cabin.

"Dr. Barnett! What are you doing here?"

Dale turned at the sound of Jenny Moore's voice. "Hello," he said to Jenny with a smile, his eyes then lighting on Lois Crane. "I'm a prisoner, too, I'm afraid. I was taken here by gunpoint to care for this fellow," he said, gesturing at the unconscious Hecky.

"I'm sorry we had to meet again under these terrible circumstances," Jenny said with a rueful smile. "Still, it is good to see you. I don't feel quite as scared."

Realizing that her fellow captives were staring at each other, Jenny explained, "Oh, this is Lois Crane, Doctor. Lois, this is Dr. Dale Barnett."

Lois was immediately taken with the rugged good looks of Dale Barnett and he with her dark beauty. The moment their eyes met, each had broken into a warm smile.

"I'm pleased to meet you, Miss Crane—is it *Miss* Crane?"

"Yes, it is," Lois said, smiling tentatively.

"How did you become their prisoner?"

"I had the misfortune to be standing in the crowd when Governor Whitson was assassinated in Steamboat Springs, Colorado." She shuddered at the recollection. "They took me and another woman—poor Dora, who was murdered—as hostages so they could make their getaway."

Shaking his head sympathetically, the doctor said, "I'm happy to make your acquaintance, Miss Crane, but like Miss Moore just said, I'm sorry it had to be under these circumstances."

"This ain't no social club!" Gavin Brubaugh's voice suddenly boomed from the doorway. He clumped across the room and sat down heavily at the table, demanding,

"You women get that breakfast cooked. We have to get outta here. Doc, you get Hecky ready to travel."

Jenny and Lois busied themselves preparing the food while all of the men sat down around the large table.

"How are you planning to transport your brother?" Dale asked Brubaugh.

"He's gonna ride a horse like the rest of us," the huge man replied brusquely.

"I don't know how far you're going," said the doctor, "but if it's more than five miles, he won't make it. You'd best put him in a wagon—and even then I doubt he'll survive."

"No wagon!" rasped the gang leader. "We gotta hide our trail from Shoshones, Doc, so everybody has to ride horses, includin' Hecky."

"Riding in a saddle will tear his wound open," Dale said flatly. "He'll bleed to death."

Brubaugh stood up and banged the table with his meaty fist, his face florid with anger. He looked hard at Dale Barnett, and then his thick lips curved into an evil smile and he said wickedly, "It'll be up to you to keep Hecky's wound from tearin' open, Doc—'cause if he dies, so do you!"

Lois was putting the filled plates before each of the men, and when Gavin Brubaugh uttered those words, she felt a chill run up her spine.

A shadow settled in Dale Barnett's eyes. The young doctor felt that fate had intervened and had made him responsible for the safety of Jenny Moore and Lois Crane, and it was up to him to find some way to deliver them from these heartless outlaws. But he would need time . . . more time than he might have unless somehow he could keep Hecky alive until the right moment came.

When Brubaugh finished eating and stood up, he stepped behind Jenny Moore's chair and placed his huge hands on her shoulders. Jenny cringed at his touch, and her face went pale.

Leaning down so that his foul breath was hot on her cheek, he looked at her and said, "You're my woman, ain't you, Jenny?"

The beautiful blonde turned her head away, saying in a clipped voice, "No, I am not—and I never will be. I am Lobo Lincoln's woman. He's the man I'm going to marry."

Brubaugh straightened up and laughed heartily. "Gonna be rather difficult marryin' this Lincoln fella when you're with me."

Looking up at him with a spark in her eyes, Jenny said with conviction, "Lobo will come after me, you can bet your life on it! And you're going to be one sorry man when he gets through with you!"

Brubaugh laughed again, sank his fingers into Jenny's hair, and held her head while he planted a kiss on her mouth. A sound of revulsion began deep in Jenny's throat, escaping in a pitiful whine.

Dale Barnett leaped to his feet, anger etched on his face, but before he could make a move, three cocked revolvers were aimed at him. Herman Tarver, Fred Foss, and R. W. Moffitt were looking at him threateningly, and the young doctor froze.

Releasing Jenny, Brubaugh turned to Dale and growled, "What are *you* so upset about, Doc? You ain't Lobo Lincoln."

The doctor set his jaw and said, "That's beside the point. Miss Moore is a fine, decent young woman. She doesn't deserve to be treated with such disrespect."

Jenny leaped from her chair and ran to the crude sink. She spat in it, then drew a cup of water from the bucket and rinsed out her mouth. Wiping her mouth with the back of her hand, she glared at Gavin Brubaugh across the room.

Lois ran to her side and put her arm around her. "I'm sorry, Jenny," she whispered.

The outlaw leader pointed a stiff forefinger at Dale and growled, "If I want to kiss my woman, it ain't no business of yours, Doc, understand? Your only business from here on is to take care of my little brother and keep him alive. And I'm remindin' you again . . . if he dies, *you* die!"

Leaving the doctor to digest his warning, Brubaugh

stormed over to Jenny and declared, "And I don't rightly appreciate you spittin' and wipin' my kiss off your lips, honey—so I'm gonna give you another one. If you do that again, ol' Gavin's gonna be mad. And believe me, you don't want to see me mad. Ask my mean ol' ma who's out there lyin' in the dirt what I'm like when I'm mad."

Jenny was trembling as he elbowed Lois out of the way, held her with his viselike arms, and kissed her again. When he released her, Jenny's stomach rolled over, and she thought she was going to lose her breakfast. Only the fear of what the outlaw might do kept that from happening.

Looking down at her, Brubaugh grinned and said, "See there, honey? That was mighty sweet, wasn't it? You'll see. The longer you know me, the better you'll like me. It won't be long till you'll come around beggin' for my kisses."

Jenny's face stiffened with loathing, but she held her tongue.

Releasing her, Brubaugh said, "Okay, you women go get your things out of the bedroom. We're pullin' outta here."

Ten minutes later, as the brightening day dispelled the shadows across the clearing surrounding the cabin, Jenny Moore, Lois Crane, and Dr. Dale Barnett were forced to ride northward into the dense forest with the outlaws. Looking at the barely conscious Hecky Brubaugh riding doubled over in his saddle, the doctor wondered how long it would be until the wound would bleed profusely again.

Except for the twittering of birds and the soft morning breeze rustling the trees, silence settled over the clearing. The cold forms of Ma Brubaugh, U.S. Marshal Patrick Day, and Carl Blade lay rigid in the stillness of death.

Just after dawn that morning Lobo Lincoln and Wyatt Andrews crossed the bridge some five miles south of Jackson and reined in at the spot where the stagecoach had been held up. Lobo dismounted and walked a large circle, studying the boot tracks and hoofprints. Bending down, he looked carefully at the prints made by a small, dainty shoe, whispering aloud, "Jenny!" Then he stood up and mounted his horse, looking at the ground from his saddle and, raising his eyes eastward, into the forest.

"They headed that way, all right," he concluded. "I'll soon find out if that was their true course, or they just rode that way briefly, knowing you were watching."

"I hope you find them quick, Mr. Lincoln," Andrews said sincerely. "And I hope you find your Miss Jenny unharmed."

"Thanks. And thanks for your help." Adjusting his gun belt and the sheath that bore his knife, he nudged his mount into a trot and headed into the forest, his eyes glued to the ground.

Lobo soon found that the outlaws had taken a north-easterly course. The rising sun threw its orange-red flame into the forest, reflecting off the flat, dew-covered aspen leaves. His jaw set in determination and his head thrust forward, Lobo rode with grim resolve. He was going to get Jenny back if he had to kill every man in the Brubaugh gang—and it would be a special pleasure to tear Gavin Brubaugh apart with his bare hands. At the thought of Jenny in the hands of that vile outlaw, his insides churned like a raging river at the height of spring thaw.

The half-breed's many years of tracking experience held him steadily on the gang's trail, and his trained eye made their tracks as easy to follow as if a herd of buffalo had passed through the forest. After about an hour, he came to a spot where two riders had come from the opposite direction, veering off toward Jackson. Then even fresher tracks showed three riders had come from the direction of Jackson to follow the same trail that was leading to the gang's hideout.

It was almost noon by the time Lobo looked through the trees and saw a cabin sitting in a clearing, about two hundred feet ahead. When he was within thirty yards of the edge of the forest, the sorrel nickered nervously and started stamping and fighting its bit. Lobo reined the horse to a halt, saying softly, "What's the matter, boy? Something up there that bothers you?" Swinging out of the saddle and drawing his gun, he said, "Well, my friend, if it bothers you, it bothers me."

Leading the horse, Lobo made his way through the trees toward the cabin. The closer he got, the more the animal stiffened and showed its dislike for whatever lay ahead. Just before he reached the clearing, Lobo tied the horse's reins to a tree and proceeded alone, and when he reached the edge of the forest, he saw what the sorrel was nervous about: It had smelled the presence of death. The body of a large woman lay on the ground a few feet in front of the house, and two dead men lay on the porch.

Lobo carefully cocked his revolver and, his eyes roving the area, moved across the clearing to the cabin. There was no sign of life. Halting at the woman's body, he studied the face. It matched the wanted poster of Ma Brubaugh; this was the Brubaugh hideout, all right. The woman's bulging eyes still stared vacantly toward the sky, and Lobo attempted to close them, but they refused to budge. She had not been dead long enough for rigor mortis to release its grip.

Still moving cautiously, Lobo walked to the porch and examined the bodies of the two men. When he saw the star on the chest of the one shackled to the post, he knew the man had to be U.S. Marshal Patrick Day. He wondered what might have happened to Day's deputy, for the other dead man definitely had the look of an outlaw.

Lobo peered through the open door and entered the cabin, seeing at once that it had been hastily deserted. He looked in each one of the four small bedrooms, and when he came to the fourth one, he stopped short and bent down. A lace handkerchief lay on the dusty floor, embroidered with the initials "J. M." Lobo smiled to himself. "Clever girl," he said aloud, sure that she had left it deliberately, knowing he would find it. He felt a tremendous sense of relief. Since Jenny's body was nowhere to be found, she was still alive. Breathing her name, he said softly, "You hang tight, darling. I'll find you."

Lobo holstered his gun and tucked the handkerchief into his pocket, patting it as though it were a talisman. Turning toward the bedroom door, he thought of the bodies outside, deciding there must have been some kind of strife within the gang. Perhaps the dead outlaw out there had killed Ma, and one of her sons had put a bullet in him for it. But why would they leave without burying their mother?

Lobo left the bedroom deep in thought, and as he walked into the main room, he abruptly halted. Three Shoshones stood by the front door, the ominous black muzzles of their guns pointing at him and their faces painted for battle.

One of them, wearing a full headdress that framed his long, coal-black hair, stepped closer to Lobo and pointedly looked him up and down. "I am Iron Jaw," he said levelly. "You are one of us, not a white man. Why would you join hands with the men who camp here?"

Lobo squared his shoulders, not wanting to show any sign of fear. "You are only half right about my being an Indian," Lobo calmly began. "My mother was Arapaho, my father was white. And—"

Before Lobo could finish, Iron Jaw interrupted, "Where are the others? Where is tall, fat one?"

Lobo wondered what the gang had done to incur Iron Jaw's wrath. Meeting the Indian's hard glare, he said, "I don't know where the others are. I'd say the fat one you refer to must be Gavin Brubaugh, but I'm not part of the gang. I am looking for them myself. They—"

"You lie! You were among the band of men that killed Tall Tree and wounded Red Feather," blurted Iron Jaw.

The towering man shook his head and said, "I do not lie, Iron Jaw. I know nothing about these acts."

The renegade chief sneered at Lobo. "Does the killing of an innocent brave mean so little to you that you do not even remember it?" Iron Jaw recounted Red Feather's story as the wounded youth had told it to him. "Now do you remember, outlaw?"

"I am not an outlaw, Iron Jaw. My name is Lobo Lincoln, and I am a special agent for the United States government. Yesterday the men you speak of captured my squaw near Jackson and brought her here, and I have followed to rescue her. I arrived only moments ago and found everything just as it is—including the three bodies outside. You must not detain me. They have gone elsewhere, and I must—"

Iron Jaw cut across Lobo's words by barking a sharp command for the braves who remained outside to enter the cabin. Three more war-painted braves rushed through the door.

Before the chief could give further orders, Lobo bristled and said, "Iron Jaw, as a tribal brother, you surely must not attempt to keep me from pursuing the men who have captured my woman. They may kill her. Because of what they did to your braves, you must understand that they are vile men who need to be stopped."

Breathing hotly, Iron Jaw told Lobo how he was going to have the scalp of every man in the gang, and the tall, fat one was going to be tortured mercilessly before he died.

"I will start with *your* punishment, outlaw."

"But I am not part of the gang," Lobo said desperately. "You must believe me."

Calling the names of four of the braves, the chief said, "Seize him! We will stake him out on the ground, cut him good, and leave him for the wolves!"

As the four Shoshones moved toward him, Lobo's muscles tensed. These Indians had just cause for their anger; he sympathized with them, and he did not want to harm Iron Jaw's braves. Being aware of how easily his tremendous strength could crush and maim, he took the course that would cause the least injuries.

Timing his movements perfectly, the huge half-breed bowled the braves over as they came within reach. Then he knocked down the Indian who stood next to his chief and, before any of the others could react, seized Iron Jaw by his shoulders, locking the chief's head in the crook of his powerful arm and placing his razor-sharp knife to Iron Jaw's throat. The rifle in Iron Jaw's hand was of no use to him in this position.

The five Indians scrambled to their feet, picking up their weapons.

"Put them down!" roared Lobo, holding the blade of the knife dangerously close to Iron Jaw's Adam's apple.

The braves froze, then let their guns fall to the floor.

"No!" shouted Iron Jaw, struggling to no avail against the steellike arm that held him. "Shoot him! Shoot him!"

The braves looked at each other, and then one of them said, "We cannot shoot him, Chief. Even with bullets in him, he could take your life."

Holding his position, Lobo said, "Iron Jaw, I wish you and your men no harm. I have told you the truth."

"You are half white," hissed Iron Jaw. "Why should I believe you?"

"Can any of your men read English?" asked Lobo.

"I can," said Iron Jaw. "I learned to read and write the white man's language as a boy in mission school."

Looking at the Indian who stood nearest the door, Lobo said, "Out there in the woods, straight ahead across the clearing, you'll find my horse tied to a tree. There's a brown envelope in the left saddlebag. Bring the envelope to your chief."

When the brave had returned with the envelope, Lobo kept the knife at Iron Jaw's throat and said, "Read the letter inside the envelope, Chief."

Iron Jaw handed the brave his gun and took the envelope, opening it up and reading the letter from William Kettering. His stern face softened as he placed the sheet of paper back in the envelope, and speaking softly, he said, "I owe you an apology, Lobo Lincoln. You were telling me the truth."

Lobo released the chief, and the braves relaxed. As he handed Iron Jaw his knife, Lobo said, "Did I understand you correctly? This killing and wounding of your braves took place about two weeks ago?"

"Yes." The chief nodded.

"Why did you wait so long to come after the men who did it?"

"I had returned to the Wind River Reservation to visit my ailing father and knew nothing of what had happened until I arrived back at my camp. My braves and I set out immediately on the gang's trail."

"I understand," Lobo said. Taking the envelope from Iron Jaw's hand, he continued, "I'll be on my way now. Perhaps we will meet again if these men go to trial. Your brave, Red Feather, can testify that Gavin Brubaugh murdered his friend."

Iron Jaw pondered the situation, and then suddenly he pointed the rifle in his hand at Lobo's chest, cocking the hammer. "Hold your weapons on him," Iron Jaw commanded his braves, who were as shocked as Lobo but did as they were told. "I am sorry to have to do this, my brother," the chief said to the giant half-breed as he disarmed him, "but your white man's law will not punish those wicked men fast enough or severely enough. You must be detained long enough for us to reach the outlaws first. Please do not make an attempt to escape, or my braves will be forced to end your life."

The Shoshone chief left Lobo's weapons on the cabin porch and then had his men walk the half-breed to the edge of the clearing. Forcing Lobo to put his back up against a pine tree roughly a foot in diameter, they pulled his hands behind him and lashed them securely together.

Standing before him, the chief said, "It will take you a day or so to free yourself, Lobo Lincoln. This will give me time to overtake the gang first." He paused and added, "I am sorry it has to be this way, for I do not mean you any harm."

"You'd best not do this," warned Lobo. "You saw the letter; I'm an agent of the United States government. It's bad enough that you left the reservation, breaking the Shoshone treaty with the whites, but to hinder a government agent from doing his duty is a serious crime. This will intensify the Army's search for you."

Ignoring Lobo's firm words, Iron Jaw mounted his

pinto and his braves followed suit. As they started to ride away, Lobo called, "Iron Jaw!"

The chief drew rein and looked back over his shoulder.

"I have one request," said Lobo.

Without speaking, the chief waited impassively for Lobo to continue.

"My woman's name is Jenny Moore. She is very beautiful and has hair like silken sunshine. Since she has done nothing to the Shoshone, I am asking you to set her free."

Iron Jaw's mouth showed the faint shadow of a smile. "I will set her free," he said. Then, driving his heels into the pinto's sides, the renegade chief led his braves northward into the forest and disappeared from sight.

Chapter Nine

Lobo Lincoln felt a wave of despair wash over him as he tried to move his wrists behind the tree. The Shoshones had cinched the rope tight, ruling out the possibility of working it up and down against the bark to wear it thin. There was not even enough slack to allow him to slide down and sit. The only thing he could do was twist against the rope until it became loose enough to pull his hands free. Iron Jaw was right: It would take him at least a day.

Patiently, he worked his wrists, stretching the tightly woven hemp strands with all his might. The rope burned his skin, and the exertion made his arms and shoulders ache, but he doggedly kept at it.

Time seemed to crawl. The sun's slow arc through the sky seemed endless. While the big man strained against the rope that held him fast, he thought of Jenny. Had Gavin Brubaugh put his filthy hands on her? Had she resisted and been beaten for her effort? How long would he let her live? Where was he taking her?

Hatred for Brubaugh surged through Lobo, violent and unrelenting. Along with it, he felt a venomous anger toward Iron Jaw for hindering his efforts to locate and free the woman he loved from the hands of the gang. But the hatred and the anger only intensified his effort to loosen the contemptible rope that was keeping him from Jenny. His wrists seemed to be on fire, but he stayed with it tenaciously.

The sun crept to its zenith in the cloudless sky and

seemed to look down upon him and mock him, for he felt
that he was making no headway. Jenny was getting farther
and farther away, and he was held just as securely as he
had been when Iron Jaw first rode off. Sweat beaded his
dark face, and soon thirst began to torment him as the
extreme physical exertion and the loss of moisture from
his body took its toll. But Lobo ceased his efforts only
occasionally to ease the pain in his arms, shoulders, and
back.

It was late afternoon when he had the first hint of
progress. As he gritted his teeth and strained against the
rope, he felt something give. At first he thought it was his
imagination, but after resting for a few moments, he worked
his burning wrists and found that there was definitely
more play than before. Encouraged, he labored harder in
spite of the pain.

By the time night fell, the rope was looser yet. He
was finally able to inch his way down the trunk of the pine
and sit on the ground, dreading the long night that he
must spend in that painful, awkward position.

Lobo was totally exhausted. His back, shoulders, and
arms ached horribly, and his wrists were rings of fire.
Running his tongue over his dry lips, he let his hatred for
Gavin Brubaugh and his fury at Iron Jaw supplant the
pain. When the sharpness of his torment had subsided, he
let his thoughts drift to Jenny, and the sweetness of her
memory soothed him until he was able to fall asleep.

Although Lobo awoke several times during the night,
he was sleeping soundly when the bright sun brought him
rudely back into his world of suffering. His joints and
limbs were stiff and hurt worse than ever. The burning in
his wrists had eased greatly through the night, but this
would be short-lived. He tried not to think of the growing
torment from his full bladder or of his bone-dry mouth.
Instead he concentrated all his energy into working his
way back up to a standing position. He had to begin his
task again.

Bracing himself for the pain that was to come, Lobo
went to work on the rope. He was surprised at how much

of his strength had returned. Fixing his mind on Jenny, he twisted, pushed, and pulled with astounding persistence.

Lobo thought of his sorrel behind him in the forest. The poor animal had been able to eat only the grass it could reach from its tether. He had noticed a ripped sack of grain in a storeroom inside the house, and he could hear the faint gurglings of a stream somewhere nearby. The horse would have feed and water first thing, as soon as he got loose.

The big man had not been working on the rope more than an hour when he felt it loosen more, and his heart quickened pace. The painful effort was paying off.

Laboring with new hope, Lobo strained all the harder, rubbing the now slack rope up and down against the rough bark of the pine. He kept at it for almost two straight hours before his concentration was broken by the sound of rifle shots. He stopped, lifting his head. The gunfire had come from behind him, to the west. He thought of shouting for help but realized that the shots had been at least a half mile away. There was no way he could make himself heard at that distance, and he needed to conserve whatever energy he had for the chore at hand.

Concentrating again, Lobo went back to his task with all his might. Sweat was running into his eyes when he heard his frightened sorrel nicker behind him in the woods. Catching sight of movement in the forest to his right, he heard a rustling of brush and a snapping of twigs, then a deep roar. All at once a massive black bear emerged from the trees, two bullet holes in its body oozing blood. Wounded in the chest and left shoulder, the beast was crazed with pain.

Lobo braced himself against the tree and froze. Lumbering into the clearing, the bear roared again, swinging its head back and forth. Lobo strained against the rope, but though its hold on him was much looser, it still kept him imprisoned. The big man fought the rising panic welling up within him. If the wounded, maddened brute spotted him bound helplessly to the tree, it would attack, and Lobo Lincoln would be torn to pieces.

But the bear saw the body of Bess Brubaugh and

began venting its fury on it. Roaring wildly, the massive beast tore the corpse apart, ripping off chunks of flesh and slashing the body to pieces.

While the bear was distracted, Lobo worked on the rope with all his might, and it gave some more but still refused to release him. He could feel the moisture of his own blood, warm and sticky on his hands.

The pain-crazed bear then noticed the two dead men on the cabin porch and flung itself onto Carl Blade's body, tearing the flesh of the dead outlaw from its bones. All the while, the blood continued to spurt from the beast's two deep wounds, staining the glossy black fur with dripping crimson.

Straining every nerve and muscle, Lobo jerked, pulled, and twisted against his bonds. The rope slackened a bit more, but still he could not pull the heel of either hand through the stubborn coils of bloody hemp.

Then the bear gave a mighty roar, and Lobo's heart missed a beat. He jerked his head toward the porch, sure that he would see the animal coming for him. It was with immense relief that he saw that the beast had discovered the corpse of Marshal Patrick Day tied to the post and was mauling it.

Lobo's heart drummed against his rib cage, and his body ached so badly that he had to force himself to continue his efforts, but his hands were almost free.

Then the bear turned and saw him. With another fierce roar, it rose up on its hind legs, exposing the bleeding wound in its chest. The animal, now a bloodied mass of black fur, dropped to all fours and bounded furiously toward the pine tree to which Lobo was tied, flashing its sharp, deadly fangs.

Lobo froze. A fleeting picture of Jenny flashed through his mind as panic knifed his heart and the horror of the moment shot bile into his throat. In one final desperate effort, the big man bowed himself and pulled with all his might against the rope that held him to the tree. He felt the bloody hemp slacken, give some more, and then suddenly his hands were free!

The beast closed in, rising to its hind legs to lash out

with its powerful claws. Saliva spewed from its mouth as it roared and swung at the object of its wrath. Lobo ducked a deadly paw aimed for his head, and the bear's splayed claws ripped bark from the tree where Lobo's head had been a split second before.

He was rolling away when the bear's huge paw connected with his left shoulder and sent a spasm of pain shooting down his arm and across his upper back. Clenching his teeth, he managed to get to his feet, remembering the gun and knife that were lying on the porch just a few yards away. If he could only get to them . . .

Filling the forest with its thunderous voice, the bear turned and charged the dark-skinned man. Lobo found that his body was still too stiff and cramped for him to run. Trapped in the awkward position against the tree for too long, his normally nimble legs gave way, and he stumbled.

Instantly the bear was on top of him, gnashing at him with bared fangs. But the teeth hissed harmlessly past Lobo's head as he twisted and jammed a thumb into the bear's right eye. The beast howled with pain, infuriated even more.

For what seemed an eternity, Lobo wrestled the maddened beast. He was soaked with the bear's blood, but he took it as a blessing, for the more blood it lost, the weaker it became. Finally he broke free again and made another attempt to reach his gun, but the snarling beast caught him before he could reach the porch. As its massive arms pulled Lobo toward its bleeding breast, he felt as though he were being drawn into the jaws of a giant vise. In desperation he drove his fingers into the bullet hole in the bear's chest. Clawing into the wound, he ripped it open.

The beast screamed wildly and fell onto Lobo, its strength waning. But the struggle had taken its toll on Lobo's strength as well, and he could not free himself from the weight of the bear. Somehow he had to avoid those deadly claws and fangs and kill the beast with his bare hands—and he had to do it quickly.

His adrenalin flowing, Lobo reached out with both hands and clamped a steellike hold on the animal's head and jaw. Gritting his teeth, he twisted the huge head violently.

With a loud crack the spinal cord and vertebrae snapped, and the massive beast went limp, falling across Lobo's legs.

Having expended his last ounce of strength, Lobo sank to the ground, his chest heaving and his head spinning. After several minutes he managed to sit up and look himself over. He was smeared with blood, but most of it was the bear's. Miraculously, he had received only a few slashes from the bear's claws, and even those were not too deep. Taking a deep breath, he began to work himself free. Finally pulling his legs loose, he rose to his knees, but dizziness overtook him again and the forest seemed to whirl around him.

He remembered seeing a bucket of water in the cabin; if only he could get to it. . . . Straining to rise, he got to his feet, but the earth seemed to roll like waves under his feet. Suddenly a swirling black vortex overtook him, drawing him into its dark void.

Lobo Lincoln regained consciousness to the sound of male voices. More like a distant buzzing at first, they gradually became more distinct. There seemed to be three men talking, and one of the voices was familiar, although Lobo could not place where he had heard it.

Opening his eyes, he looked up and saw three blurred faces hovering over him. A groan came from his lips as he moved his body; something was wrong with his arms and legs. Suddenly he realized that his wrists and his ankles were bound.

The familiar voice said, "Looks like this half-breed scum is finally comin' to, boys."

Lobo blinked his eyes and focused on the face of the man who had spoken. The man had an evil grin and colorless eyes. Then Lobo saw the purple-stumped wrist, and his mind flashed back to the Elkhorn Saloon in Jackson. Manfred Smith!

Smith drew back a foot and drove it hard into Lobo's rib cage, and pain racked his exhausted body.

"Remember us, red man?" Smith asked with a whine. "You killed our friend." Kicking him again, he hissed, "Remember?"

"Yeah." Lobo coughed. "I remember."

Eyes bulging with wild pleasure, the little man said, "Now it's our turn, scum! We're gonna help you exit this world nice and tidy. Ain't we boys?"

"That's right, boss."

Lobo looked over at Smith's two cohorts. They were leaning on shovels beside a large pile of dirt. He squinted and looked closer. They were digging a . . . *his* grave!

"Sure was nice of the folks who lived here before to leave these shovels out in the shed for us to use, wasn't it?" Smith said, leering viciously.

Lobo felt completely hopeless. His mind racing, he wondered why these men would go to the trouble to dig his grave. Clearly they were going to kill him, but what did they care whether he was buried or not?

Kneeling in front of Lobo, Smith riveted the big man with his pale eyes. "It certainly was neighborly of you to finish off our bear for us, redskin," Smith said. "Yes siree, I didn't know quite how to thank you." He then laughed evilly. "Then I told myself, now wait just a second, I *do* know how. Seein' as how you were one bloody mess after tanglin' with that critter, I reckon you were surely mortally wounded. So bein' neighborly myself, I decided to give you a good, decent burial so's your bones ain't picked apart by coyotes and such. After all, you're as good as dead, anyhow."

Lobo swallowed hard. They were going to bury him alive! He had never faced anything as terrible as this. He thought of Jenny and hoped that if somehow she were rescued from the Brubaugh gang, she would be able to learn why he had not been the one to find her.

Smith stood up and barked at his men, "Hurry up, you two! We need to skin that bear and keep movin' north to Montana."

"There's lots of rocks in this ground, boss," one of them said defensively. "Some of 'em's as big as cabbages. Makes for pretty tough diggin'."

Walking over to the grave, Smith looked into it and said, "Yeah, I guess you're right. Well, this should be good enough. When we put this stinkin' savage in it, there'll be a couple feet of dirt on top of him. That'll be enough to do the job. Ain't no way even an Indian can breathe under two feet of dirt. Go and get him."

The men took hold of Lobo by his shoulders and dragged him over the rocky ground to the grave. Lobo knew it was of no use to try to fight them; his bonds rendered him helpless.

"Okay, boys," laughed the little man with the stumped wrist. "Throw him in and cover him up. We've got to load up and ride."

Aligning Lobo alongside the grave, the men gave his back a shove with their feet, and the half-breed fell face-down into the hole.

Smith laughed fiendishly, saying, "You are about to become what that expression says is the only good Indian—a dead one!" With a flip of his hand, Smith then snapped at his friends, "Cover him up—and be quick about it."

The two men hurriedly shoveled the pile of dirt and rocks on top of Lobo Lincoln, starting with his legs. Loving life as much as any man and wanting to hold onto it as long as possible, Lobo drew a deep breath while he still could. When the first shovelful fell next to his face, he felt a large rock tumble in and rest next to his nose and chin. Then he heard another one roll in and clunk against the first rock.

As the dirt and rocks continued to pile in, he closed his eyes and pictured Jenny. His dreams of being her husband and the father of her children were about to die with him.

He listened to the scrape of shovel against rock and felt the pressure growing heavier on his body. Pressing his lips tight, he doggedly held the air in his lungs. After a few moments, he could barely hear the shovels, but the weight continued to increase. Then the sound of the shovels stopped.

His lungs began to hurt, yearning for release. Soon they felt as if they were on fire, and his heart pounded like a trip hammer. Finally he let out a little air but he held in the rest. Seconds passed, and then he let it all go. This was the end. Now he would die.

Instinctively he pulled for air—and to his amazement he got some! He let it out and drew in more. The weight of the dirt on his back was not hindering the swell of his upper body as he breathed.

Lobo realized that the air he was breathing was not just a tiny pocket from around the big rock next to his face; apparently other rocks had fallen so as to leave an air passage from overhead. He was sure of it when he suddenly heard the voices of the three men, laughing among themselves while they were no doubt cutting up the bear.

Thankful to still be alive, Lobo uttered a prayer of gratitude to the Great Spirit of his mother's people. He then tried to calculate the weight of the dirt on top of him. As he thought about it, the grave did not seem to be the two-foot depth that Manfred Smith had demanded, and he realized that the men had forgotten to allow for the bulk of Lobo's body. He doubted that more than fourteen or fifteen inches of dirt was covering him. When Smith and his friends were gone, he could make his escape.

Biding his time and breathing carefully, he listened to the muted world above him. Time dragged by slowly, and it seemed that the men would never leave.

A good two hours had passed by the time Lobo heard the men finally mount up and ride away. After waiting for nearly half an hour more to be sure that his would-be killers were gone, he took a deep breath and struggled to pull his knees up under him. It was difficult at first, but success came after a few minutes. He felt the dirt roll from his back as he pushed himself upward, and then he broke free of his grave and sat on his knees, taking a deep breath of the sweet, fresh air and opening his eyes. Dirt clung to his bloodied clothing and his face, even his eyelashes. But with his hands bound, all he could do was shake his head, dislodging some of it.

He rose to his feet and looked over at the porch; incredibly, his weapons were still there. He decided that the men had not wanted to go too near the house and the carnage of the three corpses that the bear had left. They must not have seen the knife and gun, or they would surely have taken them. Again Lobo breathed a prayer of thanks. He staggered to the porch and dropped to his knees beside the weapons.

Leaning backward and grasping the handle of the knife, he looked for a tiny crack in the porch flooring, and then he inserted the blade until it bit solidly into the wood. Four inches of the blade were exposed, and he backed up to it and went to work cutting the rope from his raw wrists. Within a few minutes, he was free of his bonds.

More than anything else, Lobo wanted a drink of water. Brushing the loose dirt from his hair and shirt, he staggered into the cabin. Picking up the cup hanging from the bucket of water, he drank deeply, not caring that much of it was running down his neck and the front of his shirt. When he had taken his fill, the weakened man fumbled about in the cupboards and found a few stale biscuits, which he wolfed down. Then he drank more water, almost emptying the bucket.

Looking around the crude kitchen to see if the Brubaugh gang had left anything else of use behind, Lobo found some old, bent knives and put them in the water bucket. Holding the bucket in one hand and his gun belt in the other, he walked out the door. He reached the edge of the clearing, walking around the skinned, butchered bear, and as he headed into the forest, he found that his strength was already returning as he went to retrieve his horse.

The sorrel gelding was nowhere in sight. He looked around, deciding that the horse had managed to pull the reins free from the small branch to which he had been tethered when the bear had first made its appearance. Putting two fingers in his mouth, Lobo whistled softly once and then a second time, and moments later he heard hoofbeats. The horse nickered and bobbed its head at the sight of his master.

"Come on, boy," Lobo said taking the reins, "let's get you watered and fed."

Just to the east of the cabin, Lobo found the small brook that earlier had enticed him with its babbling. The clear, cold water cascaded down a gentle slope, rippling over myriad rocks and dropping into a small beaver pond. He released the sorrel, allowing the animal to take its fill, and quickly shucked his filthy clothing. Cold enough to take his breath away when he splashed in and sat down on the sandy bottom, the water at first stung the scratches on his arms and chest, but then it felt soothing.

After bathing himself as best he could, he washed his clothes and then climbed out of the pond onto the soft grass, letting the warm sun invigorate his depleted body. Putting on his wet clothes, he then sat down on a rock and pulled his boots over his wet socks. Feeling cold but refreshed, he picked up the bucket and filled it from the stream, strapped on his gun and knife, and led the sorrel back to the clearing.

He went back to the cabin and got the sack of grain he had seen earlier. Then he carried it to his horse and poured it out for him. Looking up, he noted the position of the sun in the western sky; it would set in an hour or so, and darkness would fall an hour after that. While his horse chomped hungrily at the grain, he walked over to the bear's carcass and cut a large chunk of meat. Building a fire, he speared the meat with the two bent knives and rested them in the forks of two branches. As he periodically turned the makeshift spit, the aroma of the cooking meat made Lobo's mouth water.

Sitting with his back up against a tree, Lobo's mind raged at the thought of the three men who had buried him alive. He wanted to pursue them, but the need to rescue Jenny from Gavin Brubaugh was stronger.

He shoved the three hardcases from his thoughts and rejoiced that he was still alive to go after Jenny. He wondered if he dared hope that Brubaugh had not yet forced himself on her. Wrestling with that thought as he had with the bear, Lobo refused to let it overcome him, although the idea of it made his face stiffen and turned his eyes smoky. Seething inside, he said aloud, "If that filthy devil has so much as touched her, he will pay dearly!"

Lobo turned the meat over on the spit and it sizzled, splattering him with hot fat. When it was done, he hungrily ate his fill. There was still meat left over after his stomach was satisfied, and he wrapped it in a piece of the grain sack for future use. Then he walked over to his horse and stored the meat in his saddlebag.

Swinging into the saddle, Lobo circled around the clearing until he found the tracks of the Brubaugh gang and the Shoshones who pursued them. He was surprised to see that Smith and his two cohorts were following the same trail, until he remembered their mentioning that Montana was their destination. The course Brubaugh was taking seemed to be the same.

The sun was almost behind the towering trees as Lobo rode out of the clearing and into the dense Teton Forest. The big man would trail the gang that evening for as long as there was light to see by.

Chapter Ten

Heading north, Gavin Brubaugh pushed his group hard to reach the South Fork River. If Iron Jaw should come after them—and Brubaugh assumed that he would—the gang's only hope of escape was the river. Until they could walk the horses in its waters, there was no way to cover their trail.

Except for Dr. Dale Barnett, who rode beside the injured Hecky Brubaugh to steady him, the outlaws and their prisoners traveled single file. Brubaugh was in the lead, with Hecky and the doctor immediately behind him. Lois Crane was next, followed by Herman Tarver. Then came Jenny Moore, and behind her was R. W. Moffitt. Fred Foss brought up the rear, with the two packhorses trailing on a rope tied to Foss's saddle horn.

Moffitt noticed that periodically the beautiful blonde would twist around in the saddle and let her eyes run back over their trail. The next time she looked, he said caustically, "I think your lover boy ain't comin'."

Stubbornly lifting her chin, Jenny glared at him and said, "He'll come."

From the rear, Fred Foss chuckled and put in, "When he does, missy, we'll be ready for him. I'm watchin' behind us even more often than you are. Your Lobo Lincoln is a dead man whenever he shows up."

"Remember what they say about chickens," Jenny declared, looking past Moffitt and Tarver to Foss.

"Chickens?"

133

"Yes. Don't count them until they hatch." She angrily straightened in the saddle, showing the three outlaws her stiff back.

Lois Crane rode in silence, keeping her attention on the handsome young physician. Dale Barnett had won her heart the first moment their eyes had met, and she knew that she had won his, as well. Though they had barely had a moment alone, meaningful glances between them had been more than sufficient to convey the message of their mutual attraction.

Holding his mount within inches of Hecky Brubaugh's horse, Dale leaned from his saddle and maintained a steady hand on the wounded man's shoulder to keep him from falling. Hecky was doubled over in agony. Though the travelers were only moving at a fast walk, Dale knew that the constant motion of the horse's body on the uneven terrain was taking its toll on his patient, making it impossible for his wound to heal.

The young brunette looked on with admiration as she watched Dale tending the wounded outlaw, comforting and encouraging Hecky with well-chosen words. The doctor obviously took his Hippocratic oath seriously, for although Hecky Brubaugh was a wanted man and had received his wound because of a criminal act, Dale clearly felt compassion for the man.

Lois prayed silently, asking God to deliver them from their captors. Life was more precious at that moment than it had ever been before. She had found the man of her dreams, and she wanted to share the rest of her life with him.

As the sun reached its apex in the Wyoming sky, the doctor leaned over and touched his patient's midsection. Blood was oozing through Hecky's shirt, and Dale knew that the stitches had ripped open.

"We've got to stop, Mr. Brubaugh," he called. "Your brother is bleeding. The wound has reopened."

"Can't stop, Doc," the huge, ugly man said stubbornly. "Our lives depend on us gettin' to the South Fork, and we're a long ways from it yet."

"Do you want to bury your brother before sundown?" the doctor snapped angrily.

Brubaugh was about to lash out at the physician when Hecky raised his head and said dully, "Please, Gavin. I'm bleedin' bad. Don't let me die."

Swearing, the outlaw jerked back on his reins and said, "Okay, okay!" As he swung from the saddle, he grumbled, "You got ten minutes, Doc. Do what you have to do."

Everyone dismounted, and Brubaugh helped Dale get Hecky down off his horse. Then the gang leader walked a little way into the dense trees to relieve himself.

Lois stepped up beside the doctor as he laid Hecky on the soft carpet of pine needles in the dappled sunlight. "Can I help?" she asked, laying a hand on Dale's arm.

Putting his hand tenderly on top of hers, he looked deep into her eyes and said, "It helps me just to have you near."

Lois smiled, giving him an unmistakable look of love.

Hecky Brubaugh watched them, looking from one to the other. He could see that Dale and Lois were strongly attracted to each other. Though he wanted to protest, he lacked the strength to do so and kept quiet.

Jenny was also watching the physician and Lois, happy for them that they had found each other. She thought about Lobo and how this was supposed to be the happiest time of her life. Instead, it was the most horrible, and it took all her strength to keep from breaking down and sobbing.

Gavin Brubaugh stepped out of the trees and walked over to Jenny. He put a large, callused hand under her chin and lifted her head up. "Feelin' sad, are you, honey? We can't have that now, can we? You're far too beautiful to be lookin' sad—but ol' Gavin can fix that right quick. I think you need to have another kiss."

Jenny felt revulsion start in her stomach and flush through her body. She took two steps backward and bumped into a tree. Brubaugh pressed his huge body against hers, leaning down into her face. His foul breath sickened her.

Bracing her hands against his chest, she shook her head, and yelled, "No, stop! Leave me alone!"

The man's broad face took on a dangerous look. His deep voice sounding threatening, he growled, "You're my woman, Jenny. I can kiss you and touch you whenever I want. Now, you kiss me, or you'll be sorry!"

Jenny clenched her teeth and pushed against his ponderous body with all her might, screeching, "No! I won't kiss you! You disgust me!"

Enraged, Brubaugh put a meaty hand to her throat and shoved her hard against the tree.

"Brubaugh! Leave her alone!" came a shrill command.

The outlaw leader whipped his head around and saw Dale Barnett looking up from his crouched position at Hecky's side. Still holding Jenny by the throat, Brubaugh regarded the smaller man much as a mountain lion would a rabbit. Clipping his words to emphasize his anger, he said, "And just who's gonna make me leave her alone, Doc?"

Dale was unarmed and outnumbered, but he had had his fill of the huge monster tormenting Jenny Moore. Putting down the needle he had been using on Hecky's wound, he stood up and said, "Why can't you be reasonable? Miss Moore doesn't want you touching her. Please, respect her feelings and stop bothering her."

His fleshy face reddening with anger, Brubaugh released Jenny, who crumpled against the tree, and turned his bulky frame toward the fair-haired doctor.

Icy dread swept over Dale Barnett as Gavin Brubaugh moved toward him, grunting, "You shouted at me to leave the woman alone, little man. I asked you who's gonna *make* me leave her alone."

In spite of Brubaugh's intimidating size and obvious strength, Dale set his jaw and replied evenly, "If you don't leave Miss Moore alone as she wishes, you're going to force me to make you do it."

From where she knelt at the base of the tree, Jenny spoke up, "Dr. Barnett, I appreciate your concern for me, but this madman will kill you if you provoke him. He murdered his own mother, after all, so he certainly won't hesitate to kill you."

Brubaugh looked down at the young woman and snarled, "You stay outta this!" As he spoke, he swung a meaty hand and struck her hard in the face. The impact of the blow knocked her over.

Outraged, Dale rushed toward Brubaugh. Moffitt, Tarver, and Foss gathered close as Brubaugh and Dale squared off, the doctor assuming a boxing stance.

Grinning like a cat that had cornered a mouse, Brubaugh swung a big fist at the doctor's jaw. The grin disappeared quickly as Dale ducked the blow and popped the big man hard on the nose.

Dale's punch caused Brubaugh's eyes to water. Swearing at the doctor, Brubaugh swung again, but Dale saw the big fist coming and jerked his head back. The deadly knuckles grazed his jaw but did not slow him down. He braced his feet and lashed out with a left to Brubaugh's nose, followed by a hard right to his midsection.

Breath whooshed from the huge man's mouth, and his eyes watered some more. Grunting in pained surprise, Brubaugh put his head down and charged the doctor like a maddened bighorn ram.

Whirling, Dale sank his fingers into Brubaugh's overalls and used the giant's momentum to ram his head into the tree where Jenny had been crouched moments before. The tree quivered when Brubaugh's three hundred pounds slammed into it. He momentarily dropped to his knees, but then rose to his feet.

Naked hatred was etched on Brubaugh's face as he shook his ponderous head and charged again, growling like an enraged beast. Dale stood his ground and met him with a pistonlike punch to the jaw, although the force of the blow jolted the doctor even more than it did Brubaugh. The outlaw's head whipped sideways.

Then Brubaugh closed in and sent a wild punch to the doctor's jaw. Dale's feet left the ground, and he landed hard on his back. A galaxy of stars came alive in his head, and his vision blurred, but not so much that he could not see the massive man coming down on him fast. Instinctively rolling to his left, the doctor dodged the angry gang leader, whose bulk would have landed on top of him. Dale rose to his feet, swaying slightly.

Brubaugh cursed and also stood up, a trickle of blood coming from his nose. "I'm gonna kill you!" he bawled, and then he went after the doctor again.

The giant leaped on top of Dale and pinned him to the ground, where he began to punch the smaller man with both fists.

Lois screamed. Dashing over to Gavin Brubaugh, she pounded his back with her fists.

"Quit it, woman," he screamed, giving the brunette a painful shove, "or you'll be next!"

Fred Foss shouted, "Gavin! Stop! You'll kill him!"

"That's what I intend to do!" Brubaugh gasped.

"Listen to me!" reasoned Foss. "If you kill him, there won't be any doctor for Hecky! He'll die!"

Sucking for air, the huge man thought a moment and then nodded. "Okay," he said. "Okay."

Lois ripped off a piece of her petticoat and soaked it with water from her canteen. As Dale Barnett looked up at her through his swollen eyelids, she smiled and, bending down, tenderly bathed his face.

Jenny knelt on the doctor's other side and said softly, "Dr. Barnett, that was a very foolish thing to do. But I'm extremely grateful."

Looking lovingly at the prostrate physician, Lois said quietly, "This is quite a man, Jenny."

"He's far more man than the four of them put together," Jenny declared.

The young doctor smiled up at Lois. "I suppose I didn't have to go to such extremes to have you hold me in your arms, but it was almost worth it."

Shaking her head and smiling tenderly at him, Lois was about to speak when Hecky cried out in pain.

Gavin Brubaugh rushed to his younger brother and asked, "What's wrong, Hecky?"

"Gavin," he said urgently, his languid eyes on his older brother, "make the doc finish sewin' me up. I'm bleedin'."

Looking over at the threesome, Brubaugh barked, "Get up, Doc! Fix my brother right now!"

Lois's face suffused with anger. She looked up at him and snapped, "If Hecky bleeds to death, it's your fault. If you'd left Jenny alone, this wouldn't have happened."

Brubaugh stiffened and, walking toward her, was raising his arm threateningly when Fred Foss grabbed his shoulder. "Why don't you just come over here, Gavin, and we'll figure out what we gotta do to keep ahead of our trackers. Let the doc work on Hecky." Foss, who seemed to have the most influence with Brubaugh, led him away, speaking earnestly to him.

Dale Barnett stood up, swaying slightly. With Lois's assistance, he walked over to Hecky to finish the stitching job. As they walked, the doctor said, "That beast could have killed you, Lois. I appreciate what you did."

Tears misted the young woman's eyes. "I had to do something to help you," she said softly. "I couldn't let him beat you to death. I—"

Dale turned his head and looked into her glistening eyes. "Yes?"

Before she could say more, Brubaugh's harsh voice lashed out, "Hey, Doc, hurry up! We gotta get movin'!"

Dale looked over at Brubaugh coldly, saying nothing. Shaking his head, he knelt down at Hecky's side and began stitching the wound.

Lois managed a smile at him and said, "Let me help you bandage him when you're done."

When they had finished, Dale and Lois stood up and took a few steps away from Hecky. "Is he going to live?" Lois whispered.

"He's going to die if we keep traveling."

Lois bit her lip, and fear pinched her face. "You must keep him alive, Dale. You know Gavin will kill you if you don't."

The doctor nodded silently, squeezed her hand, and then headed over to where the outlaw leader stood. After much discussion, he was able to convince Gavin Brubaugh to stay where they were.

"But only till dawn," the outlaw said. "Then we're pullin' out again."

"He really should rest longer than that," Dale Barnett stated.

"Look, Doc, you can quit arguin', 'cause I've made up my mind. And if you want to stay alive, you'd better make sure your patient stays that way."

Hecky looked over at the doctor talking with his brother and called Lois to his side. When she knelt beside him, he looked at her dully and said, "You don't want me to die, do you, Lois?"

"Of course not," she replied kindly.

"I can make it if I know you love me and will be my girl."

Lois's stomach did a slow roll as she forced a smile at the ugly man and said, "We'll talk later, Hecky. Right now you have to rest. You should try and sleep. Your wound will heal quicker if you do. I'll check on you later."

The rest of the day passed uneventfully. When darkness fell, the two women prepared supper and then washed out the pots, the skillet, and the tin plates at a nearby brook. A few hours after sunset a full moon rose in the east, and except for the outlaw taking watch, everyone stretched out in blankets for the night. Jenny and Lois lay side by side, talking softly for a while, and then the blond woman fell into an exhausted sleep.

The first watch was Brubaugh's. He was leaning against a tree, watching the full moon slowly lift into the sky, washing out the stars with its brightness, when Hecky began to moan. Brubaugh looked over his shoulder and saw Dr. Dale Barnett, stretched out close to his patient, crawl out of his blanket and get up. As the doctor rose to attend to Hecky, Brubaugh turned his attention back to the surrounding forest.

Lois was wide awake. She waited until Hecky had settled back into his restless sleep and then quietly crawled to where the doctor had just resumed his position on the ground. When Dale saw her illuminated in the moonlight, he sat up and smiled. Lois eased down beside him and whispered, "I need to talk to you."

"I need to talk to you, too." He got to his knees and took her hand, checking to see that Gavin Brubaugh's attention was elsewhere. "Come. Let's go over there," he said, pointing to a more private spot.

They made their way to a stand of small trees and sat down. Dale leaned close to Lois, the words tumbling from his lips. "This may sound awfully sudden, but I have to say it. I've fallen in love with you, Lois. I know it as sure as I know I'm alive."

The lovely brunette moved closer to him so that their faces were only inches apart. The moonlight reflected in her glistening eyes as she whispered softly, "It's no more sudden than it is for me, Dale. I've fallen in love with you, too."

Their hearts were racing as their lips came together in a long, tender kiss. For that sweet moment their precarious predicament was forgotten as the ecstasy of their first kiss carried them to a world that knew no heartache or fear.

When their lips parted, Dale folded her into his arms and held her tight. He could feel her warm breath on his cheek as he said, "Lois, my darling, we're going to make it. We can't have found this love only to lose it. Somehow, some way, we are going to have our life together."

Releasing her to cup her face in his hands, he looked deep into her eyes and said, "As long as we're doing things in such a sudden manner, I—well, I realize you don't know much about me, but . . . but—"

"I know as much about you as I need to know, Dale," she insisted.

"Then . . . then you'll not think me hasty if I ask you here and now to be the wife of Jackson, Wyoming's new physician?"

Tears ran down Lois's cheeks as she smiled and said, "Will you think me hasty if I say yes immediately?"

"Oh, no."

"Then, *yes*, Dr. Barnett!" she whispered passionately. "*Yes!* I will be proud and delighted to become the wife of

Jackson, Wyoming's new physician just as quickly as I can!"

They embraced again and then Dale said softly, "Did you say you needed to talk with me about something?"

Wiping the tears from her cheeks, Lois nodded. "Yes. Yes, I did. I've heard that sometimes sick people die simply because they lose the will to live. Is that true?"

Looking at her quizzically, he replied, "Yes. A person's mental attitude often has a great deal to do with how long he lives. Why do you ask?"

"I'm thinking about Hecky. Is it possible that he could die from his wound even if he doesn't lose any more blood?"

"Quite possible. His condition is critical."

"But, on the other hand, might he be able to live longer in spite of the traveling if he had a deep desire to stay alive?"

"I'd say his chances would be much better. What's this all about?"

Lois told him what Hecky had said to her earlier. Then she said, "I love you, Dale. If there's any power within me to help keep Hecky alive in order to prevent Gavin from killing you, I must do it. Even if it means I must make Hecky think that I love him and I'm going to be his woman."

Dale shook his head. "As much as I hate it, darling, it may be the only chance we have. I just wish you didn't have to make such a sacrifice." He swore and said fiercely, "How much longer will this nightmare continue?"

"If it means that we'll have each other for that much longer, then it isn't a sacrifice. And who knows? Maybe it won't be for long, my love," she said hopefully. "Maybe Jenny's Lobo Lincoln will find us and set us free from these foul men."

"Hey, you two," Gavin Brubaugh growled, suddenly looming over them. "What're you doin' over here alone? Get back with the rest of them."

Dale Barnett stood up and lanced the huge man with a hot look.

"Don't even think it," snarled Brubaugh. "I'm half-way lookin' for an excuse to kill you, and it wouldn't take much."

Lobo Lincoln weaved his way among the trees, following clear sign until dusk faded into blackness. He was about to make camp for the night when he looked over at the eastern sky. A large full moon was rising. *Aha!* he thought. *When the moon gets a little higher, it will light up the forest floor for me. I can keep moving and gain time on the gang.*

He ate more of the cooked bear meat while he waited until the moon was up high enough to throw its strong, cold light into the deeply shadowed forest. Mounting up, he pushed northward again, following the tracks of the Brubaugh gang and their Shoshone pursuers.

Over two hours had passed when Lobo caught sight of firelight winking among the trees ahead of him. Cautiously slipping from the saddle, he led the sorrel in closer. He could make out three men sitting around the campfire, their unsaddled horses tethered nearby. Tying his gelding to a branch, he crept quietly over the carpet of pine needles, drawing within a few yards of the men before he stopped short. He had been so preoccupied with catching the Brubaugh gang and rescuing Jenny, he had almost forgotten about the men who had intended to have him suffocate to death. Now here they were.

Though he would rather have come upon the Brubaugh gang, Lobo was not at all displeased to have met up with this unholy trio. He looked through the trees and watched them laughing and eating contentedly, Smith facing him and the other two with their backs toward him. He wanted to catch them off guard, disarm them, tie them up, and make them suffer as much as he had suffered when they buried him alive. But he knew that such outright brutality would only reduce him to their level. He was a law-abiding man, and he wanted the law to deal with these three. Yet by taking them to the nearest authorities he would lose the trail of the Brubaugh gang—and Jenny. As distasteful as it was, he would have to go around the camp and move on. To do otherwise would compromise his moral sense or cause the woman he loved to be brutally abused.

As Lobo began to move around the small clearing, he heard Smith laugh wickedly and say, "I wonder what was goin' through that stupid redskin's mind when the dirt started comin' in on top of him!"

The other two laughed, and then one of them said, "They say it takes about four minutes to die when your air is cut off. Must've been kinda tough for him durin' that four minutes, wouldn't you say?"

"Naw!" Smith snorted. "Only humans have enough sense to fear dyin'—not animals and Indians."

The trio guffawed loudly.

Lobo had to restrain himself from leaping into the clearing and strangling each man with his strong hands. But the thought of Jenny's predicament firmed his resolve to bypass the camp.

Just then his horse nickered. Patting its neck, Lobo spoke reassuringly to the animal, but he knew it was too late. The silence of the three men was a sure sign that they had heard the sorrel. Lobo held still until he heard one of the three say he would take a look. Lobo, deciding to take the lead himself, strode toward the camp.

Smith had risen and was about to step away from the fire when his attention was drawn to the dark, towering form that had materialized from the dense forest behind his friends and was moving slowly toward them. The form took shape and wore the face of Lobo Lincoln, ghostly in the pale silver moonlight and the flickering shadows of the fire.

Smith's jaw went slack, and his eyes bulged in horror.

His friends saw the abrupt change come over Smith. "Boss, what on earth—?"

An invisible hand seemed to reach out of the night and claw hellishly at Manfred Smith's heart. Pain shot across his chest and down his left arm to the purple stump as a wordless squeal came from deep within his throat. The frail-bodied man crumpled to the ground, unconscious.

Turning around to see what had transfixed Smith,

both men froze at the sight of the man they thought they had killed, and they screamed in horror.

Lobo moved closer, and the men realized he was not a ghost after all but had managed to escape his terrible grave. Simultaneously, the two outlaws went for their revolvers.

Reacting with lightning speed, Lobo's hand dipped, and his Colt .45 came out of its holster blazing. Two loud reports thundered through the forest, and the two men fell instantly, one of them falling backward into the fire.

Lobo shook his head, walked over to the fire, and gripped the man's legs, pulling his body out of the blaze. Then Lobo rolled him over on the ground to snuff out the flames that were spreading on his clothing.

Leaving the smoldering corpse, Lobo knelt down beside the lifeless form of Manfred Smith, whose unseeing eyes still wore a petrified look of horror. Clearly he had died of heart failure, thinking the ghost of the man he had buried alive had come back to get him.

The big man dragged the three bodies into the woods, covering them as best he could with some brush. Then he returned to the campfire and ate his fill of their food, adding the remainder to his own supply. Walking over to their horses, he removed the bridles, placing them with the saddles. Then he turned the animals loose.

He strode back to his sorrel and mounted up, ready to continue tracking the Brubaugh gang for as long as there was moonlight to see clearly. After another hour, the shadows became too deep, and he stopped. He would sleep until dawn and then start on the trail again.

Chapter Eleven

The rising sun displayed its golden fan-shaped rays to the east as Dr. Dale Barnett knelt beside Hecky Brubaugh and checked the patch job he had done on the knife wound. It was holding well, but Dale knew it would open up again when Hecky took to the saddle.

As Lois Crane brought the wounded man a plate of fried potatoes and bacon, she asked the young physician, "How's he doing?"

"Pretty good," Dale said with a smile, getting to his feet. "Allowing for the circumstances, I mean. A little breakfast will help give him strength. I'll go eat while you feed him." He gave her a loving look and then went to join the others around the campfire.

Lois sat down beside the bulky young man and said, "Good morning, Hecky. Did you hear that? The doctor said you're doing pretty good."

Hecky's thick lips split into a faint smile. "That's 'cause you're my girl, Lois. You *are* my girl, aren't you?" he asked, somewhat suspiciously.

"Yes, Hecky," she replied, trying to sound as though she meant it. Shifting slightly, she said, "I'm going to feed you your breakfast now."

"I won't eat unless you say you love me," he said stiffly.

Lois swallowed hard and said, "I . . . I love you, Hecky."

The wounded man's smile widened. "You're really my girl, right? Not the doc's?"

"Yes, Hecky," she said, hating the lie. "I am your girl." Plunging the fork into the potatoes, she urged, "Open wide now. You've got to eat to keep up your strength."

Ignoring her last words, Hecky fastened his dull, wide-set eyes on her and said, "Since you're my girl, you should kiss me good mornin'."

A wave of nausea hit Lois as she looked at the pulpy lips. She dared not refuse. Hecky had to be given a reason to live—and she had to give it to him.

Swallowing hard to control her nausea, she said, "All right, Hecky. But just one kiss, and then you must eat your breakfast."

Holding her breath, she bent down and pressed her tight lips to Hecky's. When she lifted her head, he was grinning broadly, and there was a spark in his formerly dull eyes. Lois desperately wanted to wipe her mouth, but she fought the impulse. Struggling against her churning stomach, she fed Hecky his breakfast.

Later, when the gang and their captives were packing up to move on, Jenny drew near to Lois and whispered, "I saw what you had to do. It must have been awful."

"Worse than awful," Lois said, "but there was no choice. I—"

"You're in love with the handsome doctor, aren't you?"

"Very much."

"I understand. If it was Lobo's life at stake, I would do just what you're doing."

"I'm sure you would," Lois replied. She sighed deeply. "I hope your Lobo Lincoln shows up soon."

"He'll come," Jenny said with conviction.

When Gavin Brubaugh gave the doctor the order to lift Hecky into his saddle, Dale knew there was no use in trying to talk the outlaw into delaying their departure. Resigned to his mission, the young doctor, with Herman Tarver's assistance, hoisted Hecky's three hundred pounds onto the horse's back.

As Lois walked toward her horse, Brubaugh grabbed her arm and, drawing her away from the others, said in a low voice, "You may be foolin' my little brother, lady, but you ain't foolin' me. You don't care nothin' about Hecky. You're goggle-eyed about the doctor."

"I'm just trying to give Hecky something to live for!" she snapped back. "Dale says it could make the difference in whether he lives or dies."

"Yeah, but it ain't because you care about Hecky," grunted Brubaugh. "You just don't want me to kill your lover boy."

"Is that so shameful?" Lois asked, regarding the huge man with a dark, piercing glare.

"Nope, it ain't shameful—just useless," Brubaugh said with a sneer. Looking down at her, he ignored the question in her eyes. "Mount up," he said harshly, and he walked away.

Dale Barnett was about to mount his own horse as Lois passed beside him. Seeing that Brubaugh had his back turned, he said to Lois softly, "What was Gavin saying to you?"

"He doesn't like my pretense with Hecky—and he knows I'm doing it in order to keep Hecky alive so he won't kill you."

"Hecky isn't going to last a whole lot longer anyway." Dale sighed. "This travel is too much for him. I've been trying to figure a way to get one of their guns, but there's no chance as far as I can see."

"Jenny's so certain her man is coming," whispered Lois. "It's just *got* to be before Hecky dies."

The procession moved farther north, the sun running its course through the Wyoming sky while the outlaws watched behind them for signs of Iron Jaw or Lobo Lincoln. The group was forced to stop several times for the doctor to work on Hecky, who had begun to bleed again, as Dale Barnett had predicted.

The going had been slow, and they were on the move at dusk when Brubaugh pointed down a gentle grassy slope and said, "There it is!"

Everyone looked ahead a half mile and saw the South Fork River starting its northeastward journey through the land.

"We'll camp in the brush by the river," Brubaugh told them. "In the mornin', we'll ride the middle of the river till I'm sure we've gone far enough to fool anyone trailin' us. Then we'll pull out and head farther north into the Absarokas. Ain't no Iron Jaw or no Lobo Lincoln gonna find us then."

While they were preparing the evening meal, Lois sidled up to Jenny and said in a shaky whisper, "If Lobo doesn't find us by morning, we're in trouble."

Jenny put her arm around her friend and hugged her. "I'm sure he must be getting close. But even if he isn't here by the time we pull out, don't you worry. Lobo can track a trout up a stream. He'll find us."

"But if he doesn't rescue us before Hecky dies," Lois said with trembling lips, "Dale will be killed!"

Before Jenny could comment, Hecky called out Lois's name. The doctor was tending him several yards away. Jenny gave Lois a reassuring smile as Lois put down the skillet she had in her hand and turned toward the injured young man.

Gavin Brubaugh was standing over his brother, watching as the physician finished putting a fresh bandage on Hecky's side. Lois glanced at him and then asked Dale, "Did you get the bleeding stopped?"

"I hope so," he sighed, "but I'm no miracle worker. It'll keep tearing open until Hecky has two full days of complete bed rest in order for the wound to begin healing."

"He'll get that once we're deep into the Absarokas, Doc," mumbled Brubaugh. "Until then, it's up to you. Just remember what the consequences are if you let my brother die."

Lois tried not to let her fear show in her eyes. Looking down at the wounded man on the ground, she cleared her constricted throat and said, "Did you call me, Hecky?"

"Uh-huh." Hecky nodded. "There's somethin' you can do that would make me feel better. Know what it is?"

The brunette's stomach lurched again. She knew exactly what Hecky wanted, but playing dumb, she asked, "What's that?"

"Another kiss."

Gavin Brubaugh gave Lois a smug look, knowing how she felt about Hecky's request.

While Dale Barnett looked on with disgust, Lois reluctantly knelt down and kissed the man whose fragile hold on life was the only barrier between the doctor and death. Standing up as quickly as she could, Lois hurried back and finished preparing the food.

Everyone ate hungrily. Then, exhausted from the long, hard day of traveling through the rugged country, they all set out their blankets and slept.

The aroma of cooking bacon hung in the still, early morning air. While Gavin Brubaugh, R. W. Moffitt, Fred Foss, and Dale Barnett were in the woods, Herman Tarver sat on a log, smoking a cigarette, and kept his eye trained on the women hostages.

Jenny stood next to Lois while they performed their usual chore of preparing the meal. Gesturing at Hecky Brubaugh, who lay under a blanket that came up around his ears, Jenny asked, "Are you going to feed Hecky before or after you eat?"

Sighing heavily, Lois said, "Oh, I guess I'll feed him first." She looked down at her hands and shook her head. "I know he's going to want his good-morning kiss. I guess I might as well get it over with right now." Wiping her hands on her makeshift apron, she headed for Hecky's whalelike form, huddled under the blanket some distance away.

Kneeling down beside him, she removed the blanket from his face, saying, "Hecky? Are you awake?"

Then she drew in a quick breath. Hecky's face was stiff and had taken on the color of cold ashes. Her own face blanched, and she put her hand to her gaping mouth. "Oh, dear God, no!" she gasped softly, replacing the blanket.

Standing up, Lois battled a rising panic that threatened to explode. She whipped her head around when she heard the voices of the men returning from the woods to the campsite. Clasping her hands together to keep them from shaking, she moved back toward the fire. Tarver was watching her closely as Jenny asked, "How's Hecky doing this morning?"

Turning so as to hide from Tarver the sweat that was now beading her face, Lois felt her throat tighten. She swallowed hard and made her voice sound normal as she replied to Jenny, "He's . . . he's still asleep."

Jenny nodded.

Brubaugh, Foss, and Moffitt approached with the doctor walking in front of them. "Breakfast ready?" Brubaugh growled at the women.

"Yes," answered Jenny curtly.

Brubaugh threw a glance toward the shapeless form of his brother and then looked at Lois, curling his upper lip into a malicious smile. "Hecky get his kiss yet this mornin'?" he asked.

Lois had wiped the cold sweat from her face, but she hoped the fear did not show in her eyes. "He's still sleeping," she responded quietly.

Brubaugh blinked, nodded his head, and started walking toward Hecky. "Well, it's time for him to wake up. You got his breakfast ready?"

Ice formed in Lois's veins. "I . . . I think he should sleep as long as possible," she said, almost shouting. "He needs his rest. I'll . . . I'll feed him just before it's time to pull out."

Brubaugh halted, swiveled, and said, "Yeah, okay, we'll let him rest a little longer. We gotta push it hard today."

Lois's heart had nearly stopped. Now it pounded against her ribs, and she inwardly sighed.

The group sat around on logs and rocks, eating breakfast. Jenny sat next to Lois, and Dale Barnett, seated beside the brunette, noticed that Lois was indolently picking at her food.

"Not hungry?" he asked softly.

Without looking at him, she shook her head.

Dale, sensing that something was wrong, glanced at

the outlaws, who were wolfing down their food. Whispering from the corner of his mouth, he said, "Something's wrong. What is it?"

Alarm showed on Lois's face as she silently mouthed, "Hecky is dead!"

Dale's eyes widened. Making sure he got the message right, he mouthed the same words back to Lois in the form of a question. She bit down on her lower lip and nodded with little jerky movements. The doctor's face went pale. Hecky Brubaugh's demise was the signature on Dr. Dale Barnett's death warrant.

His mind began racing. Somehow he and Lois had to keep Brubaugh and the other outlaws from learning that Hecky was dead. The ride up the river somehow had to be delayed until Lobo Lincoln had time to find them.

Laying a reassuring hand on Lois's arm, the blond man stood up, set down his plate, and said so all could hear, "I hate to interrupt Hecky's sleep, but I need to check his wound."

The outlaws looked up briefly from their conversation of how and where they were going to hole up once they reached Montana, but they paid little attention. As the doctor walked over to Hecky's body, Lois whispered to Jenny, "Hecky's dead!"

Shocked, Jenny flicked a glance at the blanket-covered body and then whispered to Lois, "What's Dale going to do?"

Lois shrugged helplessly, her eyes showing her inward torment.

"Behave normally!" Jenny whispered. "Let's start cleaning up."

Dale Barnett knelt down beside Hecky Brubaugh, his back toward the others. Making his usual methodical movements, he pretended to examine the wound in Hecky's side, even changing the bandage. The young physician attended the dead outlaw for what he deemed to be the appropriate amount of time. Then he walked over to Brubaugh and said, "Your brother's condition is worsening, and if he travels today, he'll die. However, I have a suggestion."

Brubaugh finished his breakfast and wiped his greasy mouth on his sleeve. Standing up, the huge man looked down at the doctor. "And what's that?"

"Why don't you leave one of your men here and the rest of you go on? Hecky has got to have rest. Your man can see that I don't escape, and we'll catch up to you when Hecky's able to travel."

"Nope," Brubaugh grunted. "Hecky's tough, Doc. He can take it. He travels with the rest of us." Turning to Lois, he said, "Get some food in him. We're pullin' out in twenty minutes."

Despair overwhelmed Lois Crane. The man she loved had less than twenty minutes to live unless Hecky's death could be concealed. Audaciously, she stomped up to the outlaw leader and said with fire in her eyes, "You inhuman beast! If it was *you* lying over there bleeding, and Hecky standing here, he would certainly have more compassion and care whether you lived or died! You heard the doctor! Why don't you do one decent thing in your miserable life and give your brother a chance to live?"

Gavin Brubaugh stared at the small dark-haired woman as if he had just seen her for the first time. His normal reaction would have been to double up his fist and punch her soundly—but Lois Crane had just commanded his respect. She was right, and he knew it.

Taking another position, he said, "If them Shoshones catch up to us, lady, you'll be a target, too. What about that?"

"I'm willing to take the chance," breathed Lois, hoping she was making headway. She prayed that Lobo Lincoln would find them soon. At best, they could conceal Hecky's death only for a few hours.

Brubaugh looked at Lois askance and shook his big head. Turning to his men, who were amazed that Lois had not been struck down, he said, "What do you guys think?"

Herman Tarver spoke up, "The little lady does have a point. If it was you layin' over there, Gavin, Hecky would say, 'No more travel till Gavin is able.' "

"Yeah, but if them Indians catch us," put in Moffitt,

"we all die. Is it right for all of us to die in order to spare one man?"

Brubaugh said, "Then, Herm, you vote we stay, right?"

Tarver nodded.

"And you vote we go, right, R. W.?"

Moffitt nodded.

Looking pointedly at Fred Foss, Brubaugh said, "So how about you?"

Foss spit in the dirt and answered, "Nobody's asking Hecky. Let's ask him. I'll vote however Hecky does."

As he spoke, Foss walked toward the blanket-covered form.

The three captives eyed each other with trepidation. They could think of nothing that would keep the gang from learning the truth.

Every eye was on Fred Foss as he bent over Hecky and peeled the blanket back. The outlaw spoke Hecky's name, then stiffened. His hand went to the young man's neck, and then Foss wheeled around. "Gavin! The kid's dead!"

Lois moved close to Dale and gripped his arm. He laid a hand on top of hers.

"You sure?" Brubaugh blurted.

"I've seen dead men before," growled Foss. "Hecky is dead!"

Brubaugh swore and stomped over to Dale, his anger pulsing through him, making his face livid. "How long's he been dead, Doc?" he shouted.

Dale could feel Lois's fingernails digging into his arm as he replied, "Hecky must have died sometime during the night."

The outlaw's anger raged out of control. Brubaugh whipped out his revolver, snapped back the hammer, and aimed it between the physician's eyes. A low growl rumbled from his throat as he said, "You let my brother die, Doc! Now *you* die!"

"No!" screamed Lois, lunging at Brubaugh and grabbing for his gun hand.

The huge man easily moved the gun out of her reach and clubbed her with the other hand. Then Dale leaped at

Brubaugh, but the outlaw sidestepped and the doctor fell to his knees.

"Get up, Doc!" Brubaugh ordered, leveling the gun on the blond man again. Glancing at his men, the outlaw bellowed, "You guys get that woman out of the way!"

Lois was trying to get up when Foss and Moffitt roughly grabbed hold of her and dragged her to where Herman Tarver held Jenny.

"Let me go!" Lois demanded, furiously fighting her captors. "I said let me go!" She kicked out at the two men repeatedly, and it took all their strength to hold her.

Brubaugh's pale eyes glinted evilly as he held the gun steady and said through his teeth, "I'm feelin' real generous, Doc. I'm gonna give you time to say your final prayers. You do know some prayers, don't you, Doc? Well, you got thirty seconds!"

"No!" Lois screamed hysterically, her voice filling the air. "Don't kill him! Oh, dear God, please don't kill him!" She twisted violently against the hands that held her fast, shouting Dale's name over and over.

A rifle shot roared through the clearing, startling everyone, and they whipped their heads around to see who had fired. The outlaws froze with fear as a half-dozen painted Shoshones thundered in on their pintos, rifles leveled.

The leader fired his rifle into the air again and shouted menacingly, "Everybody stand still!"

It was Iron Jaw.

"Throw down your guns!" he demanded.

The four outlaws did as ordered while the Shoshone leader stared intently at the seven people arrayed in front of him. When one of the braves came up beside him and whispered in Iron Jaw's ear, the chief seemed to weigh something for a moment, and then he briefly nodded his head.

Dale Barnett, breathing a deep sigh of relief, slowly walked up to the chief and said, "I take it you are Iron Jaw?"

The square-jawed Indian regarded him impassively. "I am Iron Jaw."

"Sir, these two ladies and I are not part of the gang —in fact, we're their captives. My name is Dale Barnett, and I'm a physician. I just moved to Jackson a few days ago to take over the practice of the doctor who is retiring."

Brubaugh, his face white, said loudly, "He's lyin', Chief Iron Jaw. We ain't no gang, and we ain't holdin' nobody captive, neither. We—"

"You are the one with the lying tongue, fat man!" Iron Jaw cut in, his black eyes blazing. "My brave Red Feather described you to me. You are Gavin Brubaugh. You murdered Tall Tree, and you wounded Red Feather. You and your men will die!"

Brubaugh looked perplexed. "How did you know my name, Chief?" he asked almost timidly.

Iron Jaw looked over at Jenny, admiring her beauty and assuming that she was the woman Lobo Lincoln had talked about. He watched her expression carefully as he replied, "From Lobo Lincoln."

Jenny's mouth dropped open. She stepped closer to Iron Jaw, eyes wide, and gasped, "You saw Lobo?"

"Yes," the chief said, "and he was correct. He said you are very beautiful and have hair like silken sunshine."

Jenny blushed slightly and smiled to herself.

"Then you know that I have told you the truth," Dale said. "These ladies and I were prisoners of this gang. You must let us go free."

Nodding his head, Iron Jaw said, "Yes, I believe you." He signaled to his braves. "The medicine man may go free. Saddle one of the horses for him."

Dale's smile faded slightly. "Thank you, Chief Iron Jaw—but might we take more than one horse? It will be hard for all three of us to travel with only one mount."

The chief folded his muscular arms, looked at Jenny again, and said to the doctor, "You, Doctor, may go free. The woman with the sunlight hair will become my squaw."

Jenny's body stiffened, recoiling at the chief's words. "I cannot become your squaw!" she gasped. "If you saw Lobo, you know I am to be *his* wife! Where is he?"

"Tied up at Brubaugh's cabin," came the Shoshone chieftain's reply. "I could not allow him to capture these outlaws and have them tried by white man's justice. They must answer to our laws."

Jenny now understood why Lobo had not shown up to rescue her. Eyes flashing, she said tartly, "He'll get loose. And when he does, he will follow. He will come for me!"

"Your Lobo Lincoln is only mortal, not one of the great spirits," Iron Jaw retorted. "He can follow a trail, but he cannot make time stand still. We are already days ahead of him. By the time he gets to this place, we will be back in my camp, surrounded by all of my people. If he is foolish enough to follow us there, then he will die at Shoshone hands." He paused and narrowed his eyes. "I *will* have you as my squaw!"

Jenny started shaking all over, terrified that the chief would be proved right. She knew Lobo would come for her; she prayed that killing him would not be as easy as Iron Jaw imagined.

Dale Barnett came over to Jenny and took her hands in his. "I'll get you out of this, I promise. Lois and I will go for help."

"No, Doctor," Iron Jaw interrupted, signaling one of his braves to take the physician away, "You misunderstood. You alone are free to leave. My brave Sky Hawk wishes the dark-haired woman."

Lois cringed, shaking her head. "No, please, I beg of you!"

"She belongs to me!" Dale Barnett blurted, trying to shake off the strong hands that held him. "Your brave cannot have her."

"Silence!" Iron Jaw ordered, a muscle in his jaw twitching with anger. "You have a choice, Doctor. Ride away alone, or die here."

Dale knew that the Shoshone chief meant what he said. He gave Lois a look that told her he must go along with the Indian's order, but that she would see him again soon. He nodded his acquiescence, almost dazed by what had happened.

Released by the brave who had been holding him, the doctor silently turned and walked as if in a fog to his horse. As he was settling into the saddle, he heard Iron Jaw tell Gavin Brubaugh that he and his men would not be killed on the spot, but that they would be taken to his renegade camp far to the west in Idaho, where Red Feather and the family of Tall Tree would be able to watch the outlaws be tortured and killed. Dale rode away without looking back, his horse's hoofbeats not loud enough to obscure the outlaws' weeping and pleading for mercy.

As she watched Dale Barnett's mounted figure grow smaller and smaller, finally disappearing into the forest, Lois Crane began to weep uncontrollably.

Jenny took Lois's hand. She was sure Dale would head straight for the cabin to release Lobo. Between the two of them, Lois and Jenny would be rescued. She only hoped it would not be too late.

Chapter Twelve

Lobo Lincoln had traversed Wyoming many times, and he knew the land well. Leaning out of his saddle and carefully reading the signs that Brubaugh's group had left—despite their obvious effort to cover them—he understood what the outlaw leader was doing. Brubaugh knew that his best chance of throwing off pursuers was to ride up the middle of the South Fork River's shallow waters until he found a rocky place to pull out. It would be almost impossible to follow him after that.

Lobo clenched his teeth in determination, and spurred the sorrel into a steady lope northward. He had to find Brubaugh before he and his gang got to the river.

Barely an hour had passed when the half-breed heard hoofbeats and looked into the distance. A rider was coming toward him, pushing his horse hard. Lobo reined his horse in and guided the animal off the trail into the deep shade of the forest, waiting silently as he watched the man approach.

When the man got close enough, Lobo could tell by his demeanor that he was not an outlaw. Nudging the gelding back onto the trail, Lobo continued on, smiling at the blond-haired man and then lifting a hand in recognition.

The man's horse snorted as it was reined to a sudden halt. "Mr. Lincoln! Do you remember me?"

"Yes, I do. But I don't recall your name—"

"Barnett, Dr. Dale Barnett. Mr. Lincoln, am I glad to see you!"

Dale filled him in on what had happened, and Lobo listened silently, his rage increasing as he learned of Iron Jaw's treachery. *So the Shoshone has broken his word,* he said to himself, *intending to take Jenny to be his squaw instead of setting her free. That will happen over my dead body.*

The big half-breed looked intently at the doctor and asked, "Can you shoot?"

"Well enough. But I'm not armed."

Lobo reached into his saddlebag and pulled out the two revolvers that he had taken from Manfred Smith's cohorts, handing them to the doctor. "You are now. Let's go."

Heading steadily west, the Shoshones and their captives picked their way through an area strewn with huge boulders, which had been dumped amid the rocky crags by retreating glaciers.

Iron Jaw was in the lead, with his six prisoners riding two abreast directly behind him. His five braves flanked the captives, their guns held ready. Riding side by side, Jenny and Lois constantly scanned the surrounding forest, praying that their rescuers would reach them before Iron Jaw reached his camp.

Brubaugh and his three men rode with dread clutching their hearts, and the outlaw sorely regretted having impulsively put a bullet into Tall Tree's head.

R. W. Moffitt's voice was breaking as he called out to Iron Jaw, "Chief, I beg you to let me live. I wasn't even with Gavin and the others when they harmed your braves."

Fred Foss decided to defend himself as well. "That's right, Chief, and it wasn't me or Herm who did the shootin' either. It was Gavin. You've got to listen. I—"

"Shut up, Fred!" bellowed Brubaugh. "Some friend you turned out to be, you yellow-bellied rat."

Iron Jaw swiveled around on his pinto's back and snarled, "Enough! I will listen to no more of this babble. The next man who speaks will have his tongue cut out." Looking at Moffitt, the chief said, "I will allow your death to be a swift and merciful one. You two, however," he said, gesturing at Foss and Tarver, "will suffer longer before you die because you did nothing to stop the fat one from killing Tall Tree."

Brubaugh sickened as the swarthy chief looked at him and hissed, "And you, fat one. You will *beg* to die!"

Having pronounced their fates, Iron Jaw turned his back to them.

The procession wound its way past stately fir trees and into a shallow draw, passing between a pair of massive boulders.

"Hold it right there!" shouted a sharp, powerful voice, cutting through the air and echoing off the boulders.

Everyone looked up. On the boulder to their right stood the imposing form of Lobo Lincoln holding two cocked revolvers. To their left, atop the other boulder, stood the young physician armed in the same manner.

Jenny gasped, and her heart leaped in her breast. "Lobo, thank God! I knew you would come," she exclaimed, her eyes filling with tears.

Iron Jaw, shock registering on his face, reined in sharply and at the same time leveled his rifle at Lobo. When Lobo barked at the Shoshones to drop their guns, Iron Jaw commanded his men not to obey the half-breed. Though they were in a cross fire, he felt the advantage was still his.

Remaining cool, the chief focused his black eyes on Lobo and said, "You and the doctor are far outnumbered. You will not be able to kill all of us before you yourselves are cut down."

"That may be, Chief, but you will be the first to die if there is shooting."

Iron Jaw grunted, "Then so be it. But know this: While our bullets are flying, the women may be killed as well. After all, boxed in as we are by these boulders you stand upon, there is no place for them to take cover. You may have intended to use this to your advantage, Lobo Lincoln, but it will serve a far different purpose. If you do not put down your guns and surrender immediately, my men will commence firing, and your woman with the sunlight hair will probably die."

Lobo could not risk the women's lives. Thinking quickly, he said to Iron Jaw, "The doctor tells me you have taken my woman to be your squaw."

"That is right." The chief nodded.

"You broke your word."

"Her beauty is sufficient reason to break my word," Iron Jaw countered without hesitation.

"As you can see," pressed Lobo, "the gun in my right hand is aimed straight at your heart. You, my enemy, will definitely die if there is shooting. I offer you an alternative."

"And that is?"

"If Iron Jaw wants my woman, let him meet me in personal combat. A fight with knives to the death."

Lobo knew of the chief's well-deserved reputation. Famous for his knife-fighting ability, Iron Jaw had bested and killed many a man who had dared to go hand-to-hand against him. But Lobo knew that he had to take that risk.

An imperious grin curved Iron Jaw's mouth. "I accept your challenge, half-breed."

"Then Jenny will go with the winner," said Lobo.

Iron Jaw nodded, and the group guided their horses backward until there was enough space to allow for the hand-to-hand combat between Lobo Lincoln and the renegade chief. While the Shoshone braves held their guns on the Brubaugh gang and the two women, Lobo climbed down from the boulder, signaling Dale Barnett to stay where he was and keep his revolvers trained on the Indians, and Iron Jaw climbed off his horse after making sure that his female captives stayed where they were.

All eyes were fixed on the combatants as they squared off across a grassy, thirty-foot span.

Lobo removed his gun belt, and then he pulled off his bloodstained shirt, exposing his massive arms and muscular, broad chest and shoulders.

If Iron Jaw was intimidated by the mountain of a man who faced him, he did not show it. Removing his bear-tooth necklace, he discarded his buckskin vest and doeskin shirt, displaying his own powerful and lithe body. Just as the white-ridged scars on Lobo's face were testimony to past battles, the Shoshone's chest gave evidence that he had faced many an opponent in combat.

Pulling their long-bladed knives from the leather sheaths, the two men moved slowly toward each other.

"I will have your woman, half-breed," Iron Jaw declared, his mouth grim.

Lobo waved his knife, and sunlight glinted off its deadly blade. "You will have to get past this first," he said harshly.

Like a cougar, Iron Jaw sprang at his opponent with a wild cry, driving his head into Lobo's chest and spinning free in one smooth move. As he backed away, a trickle of blood appeared on Lobo's left side. It was only a surface cut, but the Shoshone had adeptly drawn first blood.

Amazed at his opponent's speed, Lobo closed in. Iron Jaw's dark eyes flashed as he dodged and bobbed, swinging the glistening knife in his hand, but Lobo managed to elude the blade and clubbed the chief on the back of the neck with his left fist. The Shoshone staggered from the blow but quickly recovered and lunged at the big man with a high-pitched shriek. Lobo blocked the thrust of Iron Jaw's knife hand with his forearm and slammed him with a knee to the ribs, tumbling him to the ground.

Iron Jaw briefly gasped for air but was up again like a cat. In a flash, he nicked Lobo's upper left arm and then was instantly out of reach.

The two cuts Lobo had suffered served to enrage him. The man he faced was indeed faster, but Lobo was no novice at this kind of fighting. He was determined to make short work of his enemy.

The agile chief came at Lobo again, flicking his knife at him like the tongue of a poisonous snake. Iron Jaw suddenly sprang, but this time Lobo sidestepped him and ran the top of his blade across the chief's back as he passed.

Shock registered on Iron Jaw's face. The cut felt like a stream of fire from shoulder to shoulder. Enraged, he bolted in again, attempting to slash open Lobo's belly. But the half-breed evaded the angry knife and savagely smashed his iron-hard fist down on the chief's wrist. The bone snapped, and Iron Jaw's weapon fell to the ground. Thinking fast, the chief dropped to the ground and rolled, retrieving the knife with his left hand as Lobo came at him like an angry bison.

Iron Jaw toppled the big man by tripping him with his body, and then the Shoshone sprang to his feet, intending to leap on Lobo and drive the lethal blade into the half-breed's heart.

Lobo saw him coming. He rolled away from the spot, and Iron Jaw hit the ground, but with amazing agility the Shoshone regained his feet instantly. Lobo was also on his feet now, ready for the chief's next attack, and when it came, Lobo feinted and bobbed, eluding the hissing blade.

His back slashed open and his wrist broken, Iron Jaw was filled with rage. Usually by this time he had most of his victims ready for the kill, but this big man was exceptionally nimble for his size. With blind fury he gripped the knife in his left hand so tightly that his knuckles were white, and then he charged, lashing out with the knife.

Lobo was ready for him. By shifting his weight, he avoided the deadly weapon, and the Shoshone was thrown temporarily off balance. Lobo brought his own knife up and drove it to the hilt in Iron Jaw's midsection.

His eyes bulging, the chief gave a gasping, half-stifled grunt. Lobo felt the warm blood flow over his knife hand. Then he jerked the knife out, and Iron Jaw fell dead.

The Shoshone braves looked on in disbelief and horror, and then Sky Hawk and another brave pulled their knives and charged at Lobo, screaming wildly.

Still holding the revolvers, Dale Barnett fired at the two Indians from atop the boulder. He killed one of them—not Sky Hawk—and was about to fire again when the three other Shoshones turned and raised their rifles at him, firing wildly. He dropped down and fired in return, hitting one of the braves in the head. Then a slug caught him, ripping through his left thigh.

Lois Crane screamed and leaped from her horse to run to the physician, but Jenny jumped down from her own mount and threw Lois to the ground. The two of them lay flat to avoid being hit.

Sky Hawk ran toward Lobo and dived at the huge man. The other Shoshones were unable to get a clear shot at Lobo, as Sky Hawk fought courageously, but he was no match for the half-breed, and within moments he was lying dead, his neck broken.

Running over to where he had tossed his gun belt, Lobo grabbed his revolvers and fired at the two remaining Shoshones. He hit one, and the man screamed and fell, blood spurting from his chest, but the other shot went wide of the second brave, who aimed his rifle and fired.

But Lobo had jumped to one side, dodging the bullet. Then, scrambling to his feet, he fired again. This time the slug hit its mark, and the Shoshone pitched facedown on the ground.

It was suddenly and unnaturally quiet. Panting furiously from exertion, Lobo staggered around in a circle, looking about. He was the only one living in that arena of death.

"Lobo!"

The half-breed looked up and saw Dale Barnett lying on the top of the boulder.

"Brubaugh and his men took Jenny and Lois!" the doctor shouted, almost sobbing, and pointing toward the west. "We were so busy with the Shoshones that we ignored the danger from those murdering swine!"

Whipping his head around, Lobo looked where Dale pointed and saw the dust cloud left by the horses in the distance. Clambering up the boulder to the doctor, he said, "I've got to go after them before they get too far ahead. Are you hurt bad?"

"A slug went clear through my thigh, but don't hold back because of me," gasped Dale. "I can take care of myself. Hurry!"

Lobo shook his head. "I can't leave you up here," he said, and hoisting the doctor easily and draping him over his shoulder, Lobo carried him off the boulder. He laid the doctor down and then gave him his black medical bag. As Lobo reloaded his revolvers, he gave the young physician a quick look and asked, "You're sure you'll be all right?"

"Yes," he said. "Just get going, man. Bring Lois back to me!"

With the desire for vengeance roaring through his body, Lobo Lincoln leaped on his horse. *If Brubaugh thinks he can escape me*, Lobo told himself, *he's got another think coming.*

The Brubaugh gang and their two female captives rode steadily for the Idaho border. Brubaugh decided that since Iron Jaw had veered them away from their original destination, they would keep on heading west. A man could get just as lost from the authorities in Idaho as he could in Montana—maybe more so. And in case Lobo Lincoln and Dale Barnett had somehow survived the bloody ruckus with the Shoshones and managed to catch up with him, the women would serve him well as hostages. The big half-breed would never do anything to endanger Jenny Moore's safety, so Brubaugh could always keep one step ahead of him. Eventually he would best the half-breed, and the minute he was safely in the clear, he would have his way with that beautiful blonde.

By afternoon they had reached the crest of the nearly ten-thousand-foot Togwotee Pass. When they stopped to give their horses a rest, Fred Foss and R. W. Moffitt nervously tried to make reparation to Brubaugh for attempting to save their own skins. The outlaw leader had already made up his mind to kill the two men who had turned their backs on him to preserve themselves, but right now he needed them. Justice would come after he had eluded whichever parties would be after him. Feigning forgiveness, he told them he understood.

Once again in the hands of the vile outlaws, Jenny and Lois were at the point of despair. They could only pray that Lobo and Dale had somehow emerged the victors in their struggle with the Shoshones, and although they tried their best to comfort and strengthen each other, they had almost given up hoping that their awful nightmare would end.

Mounting up again, the procession headed down the southwestern side of Togwotee Pass, with Fred Foss bringing up the rear, leading the packhorses and keeping a sharp eye on their back trail.

The majestic Teton Range was in full view on the western horizon, and a bit to their right was the sculptural form of Mount Moran, its rugged face gleaming in the afternoon sun. Dead ahead of them stood the Cathedral Group, the tallest peak of which was the jagged, towering Grand Teton, its cap lost in a mass of clouds and its image reflected in the blue waters of Jenny Lake, near its base.

The travelers found the harsh, rugged terrain slow going, and it took them many hours to reach the bottom of Togwotee Pass. Brubaugh wanted to lead the group farther before they camped for the night, but it was already getting too late. In the morning they would head for Jackson Lake, he decided, go around its shoreline to the western side, and then make tracks for Idaho.

The sun had dipped behind the Tetons by the time they came upon a small clearing in the forest and Brubaugh called for a halt. He commanded Moffitt and Foss to gather firewood and make a campfire, and to Herman Tarver he said, "Herm, we could use some supper. Why don't you go and flush somethin' out of the brush before it gets too dark?"

Tarver nodded and said, "I saw some small deer about half a mile or so back. I'll go bag me one." Swinging into the saddle, he pointed the horse's nose back from where they came and touched his spurs to its flanks.

Lumbering over to where Jenny and Lois were laying rocks in a small circle for the campfire, Brubaugh looked down at the blonde and smiled lustfully. "We ain't had no time yet for lovin', honey," he said, "but when this chase is over, we'll have all the time in the world. You're *my* woman now, and you might as well get used to the idea."

When Jenny did not look up or answer, Brubaugh laughed evilly and walked away.

Lobo Lincoln looked up at the sky from the base of the Togwotee Pass. He had hoped the sky would stay clear so he could continue his pursuit after dark by moonlight, but heavy clouds were fast moving in.

Pushing on, Lobo was dismayed at how quickly the light was fading. Night was beginning to gather when he spotted a rider picking his way stealthily across a meadow less than a hundred yards away. Some inner sense told him it was one of Gavin Brubaugh's men.

Angling his horse so as not to be seen by the rider, he swiftly cut down the distance between them. Moving into the trees, he made a circle and dismounted in the deep shadows. The man was carrying a rifle and looking in every direction, and Lobo assumed he was hunting for game.

The rider headed straight for him, and when he drew within thirty yards, Lobo knew for sure he was one of the outlaw gang. That meant they were camped somewhere in the area. But where? How far away? He would soon find out.

The deer Herman Tarver had spotted earlier had vanished. Not wanting to face Brubaugh without meat for supper, he had ridden farther east, but he still saw no sign of game. Swearing at the fading light, he crossed a broad meadow, heading back toward the camp. He was drawing near the tree line when something moved along its edge in the deep shadows.

The creature emerged from the shadows, and Tarver's heart leaped in his chest. It was a bear. But even before he could raise his rifle, he realized that it was not a bear; it was an enormous man, holding a gun on him. Lobo Lincoln!

"Throw down the rifle!" commanded Lobo sharply. "You're going to tell me where your camp is."

The rifle Tarver held in his right hand was fully cocked in case he spotted any game, and he was not about to give in. "Okay, okay," he said, acting as if to obey. Then he suddenly swung the muzzle toward the big man and pulled back on the horse's rein to get a clearer shot.

Lobo fired his revolver, and at the same instant it roared, Tarver's horse reared, and the bullet struck the animal in the neck. The outlaw's own shot went wild as the horse dropped underneath him.

Leaping from the saddle, Tarver steadied himself on his feet and levered another cartridge into the chamber. "Don't do it!" Lobo shouted. "I don't want to have to kill you!"

Determined to win out, the outlaw raised his rifle, but Lobo's gun roared again, and Herman Tarver fell dead when the slug exploded his heart.

The horse was in agony, and Lobo quickly shot it in the head. Furious that he had not been able to learn the camp's location, he whirled and stomped back to his sorrel.

Taking a few deep breaths to calm himself, he looked up at the sky. There would be no moon tonight, so he could do nothing but bed down in the forest and take up the search at daylight.

At the camp, Gavin Brubaugh and the others had heard the distant gunfire and figured Tarver had found game, but now more than an hour had passed, and he had not returned. Brubaugh paced beside the campfire that glowed brightly in the now total darkness, cursing. Where was Tarver? Why had he not returned?

Soon after, Brubaugh told the others that except for the man on watch, they might just as well get some sleep. There would be no food that night.

"What do you think happened to Herm?" Foss asked his leader.

Brubaugh shook his head and said angrily, "I figure by the time he finally shot somethin', it got too dark to get back here. Herm's probably the only one of us sleepin' on a full stomach. If he still hasn't shown up soon after first light, we'll go out lookin' for him."

The dawn sky was leaden when Brubaugh went out with R. W. Moffitt to find Herman Tarver, ordering Fred Foss to stay and watch the women, who were tied up as a precautionary measure.

The two captives were seated on a fallen log on the other side of the fire, facing Foss, who sat on a flat, smooth rock. Looking at Jenny and Lois, Foss sneered at them and said, "I betcha we don't see your boyfriends again. If anything, it's gonna be them Shoshones. Probably won't be as many, now, though. Your boyfriends no doubt whittled their ranks down a little before the Indians killed 'em."

Directly behind the smug outlaw, holding his finger to his lips, Lobo Lincoln suddenly stepped out of the trees. Jenny and Lois gripped each other's hands, fearful that no matter how hard they were trying to keep their faces from showing their sudden elation, Foss would read through them.

Staring at Lois with hard, cruel eyes, Foss said, "Since Jenny is Gavin's woman, honey, you might as well become mine. I'll make you real happy—just like you're gonna make me real happy."

"Lois wouldn't touch scum like you," a deep voice said from behind the outlaw.

Foss's scalp prickled and pulled tight. Like a coiled rattler, he whirled and made ready to strike.

But Lobo fired first, the gun bucking in his hand as its roar echoed through the surrounding timber and the slug entered Fred Foss's face, square between the eyes. Stepping around the dead outlaw, the big man dashed to the women and quickly untied them.

Tears streamed down Jenny's face as she flew into the big man's arms and cried, "Lobo, oh, Lobo! Thank God you're all right!"

"Where's Brubaugh and the other one?" he asked as he held her tightly.

"They went after Tarver," replied Jenny. "He went looking for game and never came back."

"That's because I killed him," Lobo said flatly.

Lois put her hand on Lobo's arm. "What about Dale? I saw him go down. Was he . . . is he . . . ?" she asked timidly, fearing the worst.

Patting her hand and smiling, Lobo assured her, "He's okay. We killed all the Shoshones, but he took a bullet in his thigh. When I left the doc, he was patching up the hole the bullet left when it passed on through. He's waiting for us."

Lois wept with relief. "Oh, thank goodness. I didn't think I'd ever see him again. Please, can we go to him right now?"

Shaking his head, Lobo said softly, "Not just yet. I want to make sure we're finished once and for all with Brubaugh. I'm going to hide you two in a safe spot, then go after him and his cohort."

"No need to do that!" Brubaugh's gravelly voice declared from the other side of the clearing. "We're right here!"

Lobo stiffened as he turned to see the huge, ugly man holding a gun on him. R. W. Moffitt, holding a cocked rifle, bolted from the trees opposite Brubaugh, placing Lobo and the two women between them.

"You should've killed Fred some other way, Lincoln," said Brubaugh. "Your gunshot brought us on the run." Stepping closer, he asked, "Any of them Shoshones still alive?"

Lobo realized that the outlaws had not heard him say all the Indians were dead. Hoping to stall and maybe get a chance to overpower them, he told Brubaugh that three of the braves were hot on their trail.

"I managed to escape," he said, "but they want to kill me, too. The best thing for us to do is team up together and prepare to fight it out with the Shoshones."

Brubaugh laughed. "Team up? You gotta be kiddin'! I'm takin' Jenny with me right now, so take your guns out of the holsters with your fingertips, nice and careful, and drop them."

Lobo obeyed, fixing the huge man with blazing eyes as Brubaugh dragged Jenny to his horse. Moffitt had Lobo and the dark-haired woman covered with his guns. Jenny was trembling uncontrollably as Brubaugh set her on his animal and then swung up behind her.

"R. W., I'll meet you at the southern tip of Jenny Lake, and then we'll head on up to Jackson Lake." He flicked his glance over at Lois and then continued, "When we was huntin' for Herm this mornin', you said you might like to have the brunette for your woman, R. W. If you want her, bring her along. If not, kill her, too. I don't want Jenny havin' to watch her lover boy die, so hold off shootin' him till we're out of sight." With that, Brubaugh put his horse into a gallop.

Struggling to escape from Brubaugh's grasp, Jenny screamed Lobo's name over and over as she and the outlaw thundered through the trees heading west. They had barely left the clearing when two gunshots racketed through the forest.

Jenny's heart sank, and she felt as though she were going to faint.

Brubaugh laughed wickedly. "Well, honey, your Lobo Lincoln is finally dead. You're all mine, now, and there'll be no one else to interfere."

Pushing his horse at a steady canter toward Jenny Lake, Brubaugh looked back as they topped a rise. Two riders were coming at a gallop. "I thought that second shot took care of your friend, but I guess R. W. had to use up a couple of slugs to fell that big half-breed. Well, I'm glad he decided to bring the woman. That'll give you some company for the times I ain't there."

Jenny swallowed hard, glad that at least Lois was still alive.

Brubaugh reined in on top of the rise. "Might as well wait for R. W. and his woman to catch up with us," he said to Jenny, stroking her hair.

Thirty seconds more brought the riders to within a hundred yards, and Brubaugh suddenly cursed. Jenny swung her head around to see what the huge man was swearing about, and her pulse quickened. It was Lois Crane on one of the horses, all right, but the man who rode beside her was too big to be R. W. Moffitt. It was Lobo Lincoln!

Brubaugh dug his heels into the horse's sides, putting it into an instant gallop. He swore heatedly, whipping the horse's rump to get more speed.

Bounding across the rolling land, the horse carrying Brubaugh and Jenny reached the Snake River. Dropping over a steep embankment, they splashed into the broad expanse of river at the shallows and raced to the other side, the exhausted horse stumbling as it reached the rocky riverbank.

Brubaugh looked behind, but he could not see his pursuers over the high bank on the east side. Looking farther north, the outlaw saw that the riverbank turned sandy just a few yards beyond them. He slid from the horse and jerked Jenny to the ground.

"What are you doing?" she demanded.

"Sendin' your boyfriend on a wild goose chase," he grunted, pointing the horse's nose straight north. Slapping the animal's rump savagely, he sent it galloping along the river. Grabbing Jenny's wrist, he said, "Come on, we're goin' this way!"

He dragged her up the rocky embankment, reaching its crest and jumping behind a hillock onto the other side. Pulling Jenny down flat, with his huge, powerful hand clamped over her mouth, Brubaugh raised his head just high enough to watch for Lobo Lincoln's approach.

Less than a minute had passed when the two riders sailed over the eastern embankment and plunged into the water. Just as Brubaugh had hoped, Lobo spotted the hoofprints from Brubaugh's horse leading north along the sandy bank a few yards upstream, and he and Lois took off in that direction.

When they were out of sight, Brubaugh jerked Jenny to her feet and started running.

"Where are we going?" she gasped.

"Where your lover boy can't find us," he replied. "Into the mountains."

Chapter Thirteen

Lifting her eyes as she was roughly dragged along, Jenny Moore looked at the mountain looming up before her and shook her head in disbelief. Gavin Brubaugh was heading straight for Grand Teton.

Jenny's long skirt impeded her, and she kept stumbling, but the huge man held fast to her wrist and pushed on. When they reached the base of the mountain, she was sucking hard for air and begged him to stop and let her catch her breath. Breathing hard himself, Brubaugh let her fall to the ground while he checked their trail. There was no sign of Lobo Lincoln.

Brubaugh pulled out his revolver, broke it open, and checked the loads. Jamming it back in the holster, he ran his gaze up the steep slope before him.

High up in the center of Grand Teton's eastern face, gleaming in the sun, the eternal snowpack sat in the gouges left by the ancient glaciers. Far below, a broad expanse of rocky tundra swept downward for a thousand feet, giving way to thick patches of alpine firs and, finally, forested moraine, where Brubaugh saw a stream of white, foamy water cascading its way toward the base. It flowed in a relatively straight line for about two thousand feet and then lost itself somewhere among the great jumble of rocks and boulders that dotted the tree-lined base. Alongside the stream, there seemed to be a natural path that would invite climbers. This was the course Brubaugh and his hostage would take.

Flicking a glance at their back trail again, Brubaugh said, "Let's go." Dragging his captive by the wrist once again, Brubaugh headed up the steep incline. They picked their way among trees and rocks and soon were climbing alongside the foamy stream.

Periodically Jenny looked back to see if Lobo was coming. Certainly he and Lois would catch up to Brubaugh's horse soon and discover that they had been led astray. Lobo's keen mind and tracking experience would take him back to the spot where he had first followed the horse's tracks in the sand, and once he was there, it would not take him long to know which way she and Brubaugh were headed.

As they moved higher among the rocky crags, the climbing became much more difficult for Jenny. The wind was blowing harder, swooping down from the lofty peaks where it lifted the frigid air off the surface of the snow-pack, knifing it through Jenny's clothing.

They had climbed up another thousand feet when, gasping for air, Jenny asked the huge outlaw to let her rest again. Easing her exhausted body down onto a rock, she said between breaths, "Where are we going?"

"I told you—Idaho," came the flat reply. "We'll just have to take a different route, that's all. We'll have to go over the mountain instead of around it."

"Gavin, we can't get over these mountains!"

"Sure we can," he said above the howl of the wind. He raised his head and looked up at the wall of granite towering above them, and then he looked down toward the base. Tensing, he thought he saw movement on the ground far below. He squinted and brought two people and two horses into focus. Lobo Lincoln and Lois Crane had returned—and Lobo was pointing his hand straight at Brubaugh and Jenny.

The outlaw cursed violently, yanked Jenny's arm, and growled, "Come on. You've rested long enough."

Jenny looked at the outlaw curiously. There was something in his voice. . . . The exhausted young woman swiveled her head, and her eyes widened when she saw what

Gavin Brubaugh had seen. "Lobo-o-o-o!" she cried. "Lobo-o-o-o!"

Echoing off the rock walls, Jenny's cry was carried down to Lobo and Lois, and they looked up and watched as Brubaugh hauled Jenny farther up the mountainside.

Turning to Lois, Lobo said, "That fool's not even thinking, and he's going to get himself and Jenny killed! I want you to stay here. If anything happens to me, get on your horse and ride back to where we surprised the Shoshones. You'll find Dale there waiting for you."

He gave Lois's shoulder a slight squeeze. Then the muscular half-breed headed doggedly up the slope, listening to Lois's call for him to be careful.

Up on the mountain, Brubaugh and Jenny passed beyond the timberline and threaded their way higher among the rocky crevices. Brubaugh looked back and swore as he saw the tiny figure far below, coming in his direction.

The angry wind whined mournfully, slamming snow particles against the outlaw and his captive as they moved steadily upward. The slow trickle of melting snow left many of the rocks and ledges wet and slippery, making the climb extremely precarious.

Periodically Jenny looked down and caught a glimpse of Lobo pressing up behind them. She had barely enough energy to keep standing, but Brubaugh pulled her along, using his own reserve of strength for both of them.

Moving higher, they reached the mountain's sheer, rocky shoulders, which made ascension all the more difficult. Brubaugh continuously looked above, picking what seemed to be the easiest route. Suddenly they came to a place where a cavernous overhang capped two huge rocks, leaving a gap of little more than two feet.

Breathing heavily, the ponderous man decided another course would be better. He was not sure he could squeeze his three-hundred-pound girth through the narrow gap. Pivoting, he started to backtrack, but then he caught sight of the angry pursuer coming on fast. Changing his mind, he dragged Jenny up to the slender opening and pushed her through.

The wind whipped through Jenny's long blond hair as

she stood on a level ledge and waited for Brubaugh to struggle his way through the gap. While he gritted his teeth and grunted, she spotted a large rock about twice the size of both her fists lying near her feet. Fear rushed across her face. Dare she try it? At this point, the monster was pinned in the gap, inching his way through.

Brubaugh saw the look in the young woman's eyes as she bent over and picked up the rock, and his face lost color. Baring his ugly teeth at her, he screamed, "Don't you do it!"

Clenching her jaw, Jenny raised the rock with both hands and brought it down as hard as she could on Brubaugh's big head. He swore at her, spraying her with saliva, and Jenny struck him again, this time breaking the flesh, and blood spurted from the gash. She was ready to hit him a third time, but the rage that shot through the huge man gave impetus to his predicament, and he broke loose.

Grasping her hands, which still held the rock, he shook them violently, and the rock fell, bounced on the ledge, and then tumbled a few feet and fell into a dark precipice. The furious outlaw slammed Jenny up against the wall and slapped her several times.

"I'm warnin' you, don't try anything like that again! If it's a matter of your life or mine, I'll toss you right off this mountain!" He mopped at the blood that dripped onto his brow, and then he dragged her onward.

Jenny had no doubt that the huge outlaw would follow through on his threat. She prayed that Lobo would reach them soon. He could handle the monster; of that she had no doubt.

After another hundred feet the going became more difficult as the ascent grew even steeper. Most of their footing was on narrow ledges carved from the sheer walls. To slip would mean certain death from a fall of dozens or even hundreds of feet onto rocky crags.

Little by little they were working their way around to the south face of Grand Teton's towering form. The sun had climbed to its apex, but the temperature was dropping steadily as they rose higher. Jenny was freezing in the cold air and the relentless wind, whose arctic blasts sliced clear through her body. Her strength gone, she suddenly collapsed. Winded himself, Brubaugh sat down beside her and sucked for air.

Looking up at him, she said, "Why don't you just go on without me? I'm slowing you down."

"Not on your life," gasped the outlaw. "You're my ticket to freedom. As long as you're alive, your lover boy won't do anything that might put you in danger—meanin' he's got to play by *my* rules."

Then they both looked back the way they had come and saw Lobo squeezing through the narrow gap where Jenny had bludgeoned Brubaugh.

Hurry, Lobo! Oh, please hurry! Jenny screamed inside.

Pressing on with urgency, they came to a rocky ledge jutting out into the air. Squinting her eyes against the biting wind, Jenny looked down into the yawning depths below, and the thought of falling sent a shudder through her body. The path up from the ledge grew narrower, and Brubaugh let go of her and said, "You go ahead of me."

Jenny was about to move on when a fierce gust of wind whipped across the face of the mountain, and the hulking outlaw was thrown off balance. Reacting without thinking, the young woman thrust her open palms against his chest and shoved him toward the edge. Brubaugh screamed as he went over, clawing at the rocky ledge, his feet dangling in empty space.

Jenny put her back against the rock wall behind her and looked on white faced while Brubaugh thrashed to haul himself back up. The intensity in his eyes was terrible as he clutched the rocky ledge for dear life, desperately trying over and over to swing his foot onto the ledge. He finally succeeded and lifted himself back to safety.

Jenny was paralyzed with fear as he rose to his feet, his eyes wild. The sharp rocks had lacerated his hands, and blood was oozing from the wounds. Furious, the huge man threw Jenny down and pounced on top of her, swearing at the top of his voice and clutching her throat, cutting off her air. "I oughtta kill you!" he screamed. "If I didn't need you, I would!"

He let go of her throat and shook her savagely, roaring into the wind. Then yanking her to her feet, he growled, "You're gonna be sorry you did that. As soon as I've got you where I want you, I'm gonna get rid of that spirit of yours—and it ain't gonna take long, missy, I promise you!"

Praying even harder that Lobo would catch up with them before it was too late, Jenny had to force herself to hope that he would rescue her in time. It was the only thing that kept her from stepping off the edge of the mountain, for she felt that death would be preferable to life with Gavin Brubaugh.

They had climbed up nearly two thousand feet when Jenny called back to Brubaugh, "We can't go any farther!"

He swore and followed her out onto a narrow ledge, which abruptly ended at a twenty-foot-high granite wall. They could not go any higher without climbing equipment.

They stood there for what seemed an eternity as the wind whipped fiercely around them. With no way to go but down, Brubaugh knew he had to make his stand—but he would do it on his terms. His mind working fast, he dragged Jenny back down to a place among the jagged rocks where, although they would be hidden from view from below, they could see Lobo when he appeared. Lobo would have to come this way, the formation of the rocks making any other choice impossible.

Brubaugh pulled Jenny beside him, and they hunkered down behind the rock. It was more protected here, and they could hear the distant sounds of Lobo's climb over the low moan of the wind. The outlaw roughly locked Jenny's head in the crook of his arm and clamped his hand over her mouth. Pulling his gun and cocking it, he hissed, "You try to warn him and I'll kill you!" Then he waited for the unsuspecting half-breed to walk right into the muzzle of his .45.

Hearing Lobo's labored breathing, they knew he was getting close. Brubaugh readied his gun and lifted his head so he could see over the rock. Helpless, Jenny wished she had had the courage to dislodge Brubaugh's hands and sent him plummeting. Her heart pounded as she realized that even if Lobo could survive the gunshot, he would no doubt fall from the narrow path into the abyss below.

The sounds of Lobo's approach grew louder; he would appear at any second. Jenny whined as she struggled against the strong hand that covered her mouth. Brubaugh gripped her harder and whispered angrily, "I'll kill you! I mean it!"

Disregarding her own safety, she twisted her head enough to loosen Brubaugh's hold. Getting a thick finger between her teeth, she bit down with all her might, and when he instinctively let go, she screamed, "Lobo! Look out!"

Lobo's head suddenly appeared, but Jenny's warning had come in time. He ducked back behind the rock as the bullet ricocheted off the granite where his head would have been. The sound of the shot resounded through the canyons.

Brubaugh instantly grabbed Jenny, who fought to free herself from his grasp, and blinded with rage, he swung the gun toward her head. He fired just as Lobo charged behind the rock and leaped at him.

As the gun discharged, Jenny fell into a shallow gap between outcroppings of rock, where she lay facedown in a crumpled heap, completely still.

The force of Lobo's leap had knocked Brubaugh down. Pivoting to meet the fiery-eyed half-breed, the outlaw tried to aim the revolver at him. But Lobo kicked the gun from Brubaugh's hand and sent it sailing over the edge of the precipice.

Roaring Jenny's name, Lobo smashed into Brubaugh like an enraged grizzly who had lost her cub. Twisting and turning, the huge outlaw desperately attempted to use his fifty-pound advantage to force Lobo to the edge, to send him to the bottom of the dark, rocky canyon.

But this fierce son of an Arapaho woman had been transformed by rage into a behemoth, making him more than a match for the bigger man. Slowly, he drove the

giant backward toward the fearsome brink, both men gasping and grunting, exerting all their energy to emerge the
victor in this life-and-death struggle.

Lobo felt Brubaugh grab hold of his shirt. The half-
breed knew he somehow had to break the outlaw's grasp
or they would both go into the yawning chasm. Digging in
his heels and trying to gain a purchase, he yanked the
outlaw toward the rock wall and swung him around, slamming his back against the hard granite.

The breath whooshed from Brubaugh's lungs, and
Lobo chopped him on the jaw with a savage blow, snapping the outlaw's head against the rock wall, stunning
him. Brubaugh slid down the wall in a heap, shaking his
head to clear it.

Hissing with fury, Lobo leaned over and with one
hand grabbed hold of the back of his enemy's shirt and
with the other anchored his fingers in a fistful of denim at
Brubaugh's rump. Then, bending his knees, he rolled the
outlaw over and, making sure the three-hundred-pound
weight was centered, extended his arms and hoisted him
straight overhead.

As Lobo inched his way to the edge of the rocky
precipice, the outlaw's vision cleared. Flailing his arms
and legs, he tried desperately to grab hold of Lobo, but
his position made it impossible. He looked up into the
vivid blue sky and over at the jagged Tetons, and then
down into the yawning abyss.

"No!" he screamed. "No, Lincoln, have mercy! I beg
of you, don't—"

His words were cut off as he was flung into empty
space. A hellish wail exploded from his throat as he plum-
meted, the frenzied cry echoing off the mountain, trailing
downward, and steadily fading until there was nothing.

Staring down into the abyss for a long moment, listening to the howling wind, Lobo felt that its mournful
wail matched the cry in his anguished soul. He slowly
turned and walked back, forcing himself to look down at
the inert form of Jenny Moore. In a daze, he climbed
down into the hollow where she lay, tears spilling from his
eyes. He crouched down beside her and, tenderly slipping

his hand under her head, turned it so he could see her face.

Lobo drew a sharp breath as Jenny suddenly moved her head and moaned.

"Jenny!" he breathed, gathering her into his arms. "Jenny, you're alive!"

The beautiful blond woman fluttered her eyes, opened them, and looked into Lobo's face. Blinking to clear the fog, she stared incredulously and said, "Darling, is . . . is it really you?"

"It sure is, honey," he said with quivering lips. "You're safe now. Really safe."

"And Gavin?"

"He . . . uh . . . fell off the ledge."

"Oh, Lobo . . ."

The big half-breed kissed his woman passionately, soaking her face with his tears. The nightmare was finally over.

"I thought you were dead," she said, still staring in disbelief.

"I thought *you* were dead. How was it that Brubaugh's bullet missed your head? He was aiming straight at you when I charged into him."

Jenny smiled at him. "I guess that's how I got shoved into this hollow. When you charged into Gavin, he knocked into me—hard! But how did *you* escape his bullet? . . . Oh! I guess I saved your life the same way you saved mine." She giggled. "No one could ever say we don't think alike, my darling."

Lobo laughed and hugged her tight, kissing her hair, her forehead, and finally again her lips. Sighing deeply, he stood up and lifted her to her feet. "We should start on our way back down. Lois will be wondering if we're all right. She'll be eager to get back to her doctor."

"You mean Dale is safe? Oh, thank goodness. I was afraid he wasn't, after I saw him get shot, back at the boulders."

Lobo smiled at her and assured her that the young physician was slightly wounded but otherwise was fine. "I left him by the rocks. He'll be most anxious about all of us by now."

As they slowly made their way back down the precarious mountain, Jenny asked how Lobo had escaped Moffitt's bullet, and he explained that he had knocked Lois out of the way and dived for his own gun, getting off the first shot.

Shuddering, Jenny stopped short and looked into Lobo's eyes. "You were almost killed so many times in the past few days because of me."

Lobo folded her into his arms. "First of all, I wasn't almost killed because of you—I was almost killed because you were put in danger by loathsome vermin. And second of all, my darling," he said, whispering into her ear, "I'd do it all over again. You *are* my life."

The sun was setting, washing Wyoming's Teton Forest with brilliant orange light as Dr. Dale Barnett sat impatiently, finding the wait unbearable. Studying the colors of the sunset as they reflected off the streaky clouds, he brooded over the fate of Lois, Jenny, and Lobo. He told himself that if they did not return by daylight, he would go hunting for them in spite of his wounded leg.

Just then he heard a horse snort, and he swung his head around and cautiously placed his hand on one of the revolvers that lay next to him. Three horses were coming his way, two of which were being ridden and the third being led.

The doctor eased himself to his feet, placing his weight on his good leg. Seconds later he could make out Lobo Lincoln and Jenny Moore doubled up on Lobo's sorrel. The other rider was Lois Crane.

Lois's voice carried to him as she called the doctor's name and put her horse into a gallop. Dale stood with his heart beating, waiting. When the horse skidded to a halt, Lois Crane was instantly out of the saddle and into his arms.

After a brief and joyous reunion, they mounted up and rode a few miles farther west, heading for the town of

Moran. They would send some of the townsmen back for the bodies of the dead, returning the Shoshones to their reservation and burying the gang members in a common grave in the town's cemetery. After they notified the authorities of everything that had happened—including Albert Overby's role in the assassination of Governor Roger Whitson—Lobo and Dale would undoubtedly be entitled to share the reward money that was posted on the Brubaughs' heads.

When it got too dark to continue, they unsaddled the horses and made a campfire, sharing the last of the food Lobo had stored in his saddlebags. Gesturing at the suitcase that was tied around one of the saddle horns, Dale said, "Well, that's one good thing that came out of this horrible nightmare."

"What's that?" queried Lobo.

"The bank's going to get its thirty thousand dollars back."

Lois pointedly cleared her throat. "I would say, Doctor, that there's something better than the bank getting its money back."

"And that is?" said the doctor with a knowing smile.

The brunette took hold of his hand, looked lovingly into his eyes, and breathed, "I found the most wonderful man in the world."

The happy foursome had a good laugh, and then Jenny said, "I figure it'll take us two days at this easy pace to reach Jackson, and I'm going to marry my own wonderful man the minute we get there. What are you going to do, Lois?"

Lois looked at Dale, and before she could respond, the doctor said, "How about a double wedding?"

A loud cheer went up at the idea, and the proposition got a unanimous vote.

The stars rose in the night sky, forming an immense, twinkling canopy over the two couples, each bride-to-be nestled safely in her man's arms, wanting to be nowhere else on earth.

Jenny Moore cuddled close to her big man and said softly, "Lobo?"

"Mmm-hmm."

"Will it be as beautiful as this at our new home at the ranch?"

"Just as beautiful," he promised.

Jenny sighed. "Good, because this seems just like heaven to me." She turned and lifted her lips to Lobo's, kissing him passionately.

Taking a breath, the big half-breed whispered, "It must be heaven, my darling, because I'm sure I just heard angels singing."

STAGECOACH

STATION 39:

FORT VERDE
by Hank Mitchum

When Lieutenant Mark Shields's stagecoach arrives at Fort Verde, Arizona, his father's legacy of military greatness paves the way for him, though he would just as soon be rid of it. The fort's residents are impressed by the young officer when he takes command of a patrol that is attacked by the hostile Apache warrior Manitoro and his men.

Later that week the lieutenant leads a patrol to find Manitoro. They stop at a nearby Indian village, inhabited by friendly Apaches and led by Chief Chatoma, and Shields is surprised to see a beautiful young blond woman living among them. Her name is Shasha Quiet Stream, and she has lived among the Indians since she was five. Shields is entranced by her quiet strength and beauty. Chatoma, who raised her, is very ill, and Shields takes him to the fort for treatment. The beautiful young woman accompanies them, much to Shields's delight.

As Manitoro's hostilities increase, Shields discovers that the renegade is being fed information about the fort. The future of Chatoma's peace-loving people is consequently threatened. Shields must defeat Manitoro to prevent mass slaughter of all Indians in the area—and as he does, he learns the startling truth about the woman he loves.

Read **FORT VERDE**, on sale February 1988 wherever Bantam paperbacks are sold.